FIRST, BODY

///

15.

Books by

MELANIE RAE THON

❮

Meteors in August

Girls in the Grass

Iona Moon

First, Body

First, Body

S T O R I E S

Melanie Rae Thon

Houghton Mifflin Company

Boston   New York

1997

For information about permission to reproduce selections from this book,
write to Permissions, 215 Park Avenue South, New York, NY 10003
For information about this and other Houghton Mifflin trade and reference books
and multimedia products, visit The Bookstore at Houghton Mifflin
on the World Wide Web at http://www.hmco.com/trade/.

Library of Congress Cataloging-in-Publication Data
Thon, Melanie Rae.
First, body: stories / Melanie Rae Thon.
p. cm.
Contents: First, body — Father, lover, deadman, dreamer — Little white sister —
Nobody's daughters — The snow thief — Bodies of water — Necessary angels.
ISBN 0-395-78588-x
I. Title.
PS3570.H6474F57 1997   813'.54—DC20   96-33088   CIP

Book design by Anne Chalmers; typeface: Linotype-Hell Fairfield

Printed in the United States of America

QUM 10 9 8 7 6 5 4 3 2 1

The author is grateful for permission to reprint lines from "The Dead Woman," by
Pablo Neruda, from *The Captain's Verses,* translated by Donald D. Walsh. Copyright
© 1972 by Pablo Neruda and Donald D. Walsh. Reprinted by permission of New Di-
rections Publishing Corp.
    The excerpt from Joan Brady's novel *Theory of War* is taken from the edition pub-
lished by Fawcett in 1994.
    "First, Body" first appeared in *Antaeus* and was reprinted in *The Best American
Short Stories 1995.* "Father, Lover, Deadman, Dreamer" first appeared in *Story.* "Little White Sister" first appeared in *Ploughshares* and was reprinted in *Syracuse Uni-
versity Magazine.* From "Nobody's Daughters," "In These Woods" was first published
as "What She Wants" in the anthology *Women on Hunting* and was reprinted in
Hootenanny; "Xmas, Jamaica Plain" first appeared in *Ontario Review* and was
reprinted in *The Best American Short Stories 1996* and *Granta;* "Home" first appeared in *Bomb.* "The Snow Thief" appeared in *The Penguin Book of International
Women's Short Stories* and *Writers Harvest II.* "Necessary Angels" first appeared in
Paris Review.

FOR THE CHILDREN:

Hayley, Christopher, Kelsey, Bradley, Michael, and Melinda

If suddenly you do not exist,
If suddenly you are not living,
I shall go on living.

I do not dare,
I do not dare to write it,
if you die.

I shall go on living.

> —Pablo Neruda,
> "The Dead Woman"

Life clings tight to its shape. Look in the mirror. Day after day, year after year, there's hardly any change at all.... And yet every bone, every muscle, every patch of skin, tendon, blood vessel—every single particle—is being destroyed and replaced right as you look. Surface calm—and a mad scramble of activity underneath.... The shape, the form, the pattern —all unchanged and yet not one single molecule of what was you seven years ago is part of you now. What do you want? Eternal permanence?

> —Joan Brady,
> *Theory of War*

Contents

F I R S T ,

B O D Y

❙❙❙ TWO NURSES with scissors could make a man naked in eleven seconds. Sid Elliott had been working Emergency eight months and it amazed him every time. Slicing through denim and leather, they peeled men open faster than Sid's father flayed rabbits.

Roxanne said it would take her longer than eleven seconds to make him naked. "But not that much longer." It was Sunday. They'd met in the park on Tuesday, and she hadn't left Sid's place since Friday night. She was skinny, very dark-skinned. She had fifteen teeth of her own and two bridges to fill the spaces. "Rotted out on smack and sugar. But I don't do that shit anymore." It was one of the first things she told him. He looked at her arms. She had scars, hard places where the skin was raised. He traced her veins with his fingertips, feeling for bruises. She was never pretty. She said this too. "So don't go thinking you missed out on something."

He took her home that night, to the loft in the warehouse overlooking the canal, one room with a high ceiling, a mattress on the floor beneath the window, a toilet behind a screen, one huge chair, one sink, a hot plate with two burners, and a miniature refrigerator for the beer he couldn't drink anymore.

"It's perfect," she said.

Now they'd known each other six days. She said, "What do you see in me?"

"Two arms, two ears. Someone who doesn't leave the room when I eat chicken."

"Nowhere to go," she said.

"You know what I mean."

He told her about the last boy on the table in Emergency. He'd fallen thirty feet. When he woke, numb from the waist, he said, *Are those my legs?* She lay down beside him, and he felt the stringy ligaments of her thighs, the rippled bone of her sternum; he touched her whole body the way he'd touched her veins that night in the park, by the water.

He sat at his mother's kitchen table. "What is it you do?" she said.

"I clean up."

"Like a janitor?"

Up to our booties in blood all night, Dr. Enos said.

"Something like that."

She didn't want to know, not exactly, not any more than she'd wanted to know what his father was going to do with the rabbits.

She nodded. "Well, it's respectable work."

She meant she could tell her friends Sid had a hospital job. He waited.

"Your father would be proud."

He remembered a man slipping rabbits out of their fur coats. His father had been laid off a month before he thought of this.

Tonight his mother had made meatloaf, which was safe — so long as he remembered to take small bites and chew slowly. Even so, she couldn't help watching, and he kept covering his mouth with his napkin. Finally he couldn't chew at all and had to wash each bite down with milk. When she asked, "Are you happy there?" he wanted to tell her about the men with holes in their skulls, wanted to bring them, trembling, into this room. Some had been wounded three or four times. They had beards, broken teeth, scraped heads. The nurses made jokes about burning their clothes.

But the wounds weren't bullet holes. Before the scanners, every drunk who hit the pavement got his head drilled. "A precautionary measure," Dr. Enos explained. "In case of hemorrhage."

"Did the patient have a choice?"

"Unconscious men don't make choices."

Sid wanted to tell his mother that. *Unconscious men don't make choices.* He wanted her to understand the rules of Emergency: first, body, then brain — stop the blood, get the heart beating. No fine tuning. Don't worry about a man's head till his guts are back in his belly.

Dr. Enos made bets with the nurses on Saturday nights. By stars and fair weather they guessed how many motorcyclists would run out of luck cruising from Seattle to Marysville without their helmets, how many times the choppers would land on the roof of the hospital, how many men would be stripped and pumped but not saved.

Enos collected the pot week after week. "If you've bet on five and only have three by midnight, do you wish for accidents?" Dr. Roseland asked. Roseland never played. She was beyond it, a grown woman. She had two children and was pregnant with the third.

"Do you?" Enos said.

"Do I what?"

Enos stared at Roseland's swollen belly. "Wish for accidents," he said.

Skulls crushed, hearts beating, the ones lifted from the

roads arrived all night. Enos moved stiffly, like a man just out of the saddle. He had watery eyes — bloodshot, blue. Sid thought he was into the pharmaceuticals. But when he had a body on the table, Enos was absolutely focused.

Sid wanted to describe the ones who flew from their motor-cycles and fell to earth, who offered themselves this way. *Like Jesus.* His mother wouldn't let him say that. *With such grace.* He wished he could make her see how beautiful it was, how ordinary, the men who didn't live, whose parts were packed in plastic picnic coolers and rushed back to the choppers on the roof, whose organs and eyes were delivered to Portland or Spokane. He was stunned by it, the miracle of hearts in ice, corneas in milk. These exchanges became the sacrament, transubstantiated in the bodies of startled men and weary children. Sometimes the innocent died and the faithless lived. Sometimes the blind began to see. Enos said, "We save bodies, not souls."

Sid tasted every part of Roxanne's body: sweet, fleshy lobe of the ear, sinewy neck, sour pit of the arm, scarred hollow of the elbow. He sucked each finger, licked her salty palm. He could have spent weeks kissing her, hours with his tongue inside her. Sometimes he forgot to breathe and came up gasping. She said, "Aren't you afraid of me?"

And he said, "You think you can kill me?"

"Yes," she said, "anybody can."

She had narrow hips, a flat chest. He weighed more than twice what she did. He was too big for himself, always — born too big, grown too fast. Too big to cry. Too big to spill his milk. At four he looked six; at six, ten. Clumsy, big-footed ten. Slow, stupid ten. *Like living with a bear,* his mother said, something broken every day, her precious blown-glass ballerina crumbling in his hand, though he held her so gently, lifting her to the window to let the light pass through her. He had thick wrists, enormous thumbs. Even his eyebrows were bushy. *My monster,* Roxanne said the second night, *who made you this way?*

"How would you kill me?" he said. He put one heavy leg over her skinny legs, pinning her to the bed.

"You know, with my body."

"Yes, but how?"

"You know what I'm saying."

"I want you to explain."

She didn't. He held his hand over her belly, not quite touching, the thinnest veil of air between them. "I can't think when you do that," she said.

"I haven't laid a finger on you."

"But you will," she said.

He'd been sober twenty-seven days when she found him. Now it was forty-two. Not by choice. He'd had a sudden intolerance for alcohol. Two shots and he was on the floor, puking his guts out. He suspected Enos had slipped him some Antabuse and had a vague memory: his coffee at the edge of the counter, Enos drifting past it. Did he linger? Did he know whose it was? But it kept happening. Sid tried whiskey instead of rum, vodka instead of whiskey. After the third experiment he talked to Roseland. "Count your blessings," she said. "Maybe you'll have a liver when you're sixty." She looked at him in her serious, sad way, felt his neck with her tiny hands, thumped his back and chest, shined her flashlight into his eyes. When he was sitting down, she was his height. He wanted to lay his broad hand on her bulging stomach.

No one was inclined to offer a cure. He started smoking pot

instead, which was what he was doing that night in the park when Roxanne appeared. *Materialized,* he said afterward, *out of smoke and air.*

But she was no ghost. She laughed loudly. She even breathed loudly — through her mouth. They lay naked on the bed under the open window. The curtains fluttered and the air moved over them.

"Why do you like me?" she said.

"Because you snore."

"I don't."

"How would you know?"

"It's my body."

"It does what it wants when you're sleeping."

"You like women who snore?"

"I like to know where you are."

He thought of his sister's three daughters. They were slim and quick, moving through trees, through dusk, those tiny bodies — disappearing, reassembling — those children's bodies years ago. Yes, it was true. His sister was right. Better that he stayed away. Sometimes when he'd chased them in the woods, their bodies had frightened him — the narrowness of them, the way they hid behind trees, the way they stepped in the river, turned clear and shapeless, flowed away. When they climbed out downstream, they were whole and hard but cold as water. They sneaked up behind him to grab his knees and pull him to the ground. They touched him with their icy hands, laughing like water over stones. He never knew where they might be, or what.

He always knew exactly where Roxanne was: behind the screen, squatting on the toilet; standing at the sink, splashing water under her arms. Right now she was shaving her legs, singing nonsense words, *Sha-na-na-na-na*, like the backup singer she said she was once. "The Benders — you probably heard of them." He nodded but he hadn't. He tried to picture her twenty-four years younger, slim but not scrawny. Roxanne with big hair and white sequins. Two other girls just like her, one in silver, one in black, all of them shimmering under the lights. "But it got too hard, dragging the kid around — so I gave it up." She'd been with Sid twenty-nine days and this was the first he'd heard of any kid. He asked her. "Oh yeah," she said, "of course." She gave him a look like, *What d'you think — I was a virgin?* "But I got smart after the first one." She was onto the second leg, humming again. "Pretty kid. Kids of her own now. I got pictures." He asked to see them, and she said, "Not *with* me."

"Where?" he said.

She whirled, waving the razor. "You the police?"

She'd been sober five days. That's when the singing started. "If you can do it, so can I," she'd said.

He reminded her he'd had no choice.

"Neither do I," she said, "if I want to stay."

He didn't agree. He wasn't even sure it was a good idea. She told him she'd started drinking at nine: stole her father's bottle and sat in the closet, passed out and no one found her for two days. Sid knew it was wrong, but he was almost proud of her for that, forty years of drinking — he didn't know anyone else who'd started so young. She had conviction, a vision of her life, like Roseland, who said she'd wanted to be a doctor since fifth grade.

Sid was out of Emergency. Not a demotion. A lateral transfer. That's what Mrs. Mendelson in personnel said. Her eyes and half her face were shrunken behind her glasses.

"How can it be lateral if I'm in the basement?"

"I'm not speaking literally, Sid."

He knew he was being punished for trying to stop the girl from banging her head on the wall.

Inappropriate interference with a patient. There was a language for everything. *Sterilized equipment contaminated.*

Dropped — he'd dropped the tray to help the girl.

"I had to," he told Roxanne.

"Shush, it's okay — you did the right thing."

There was no reward for doing the right thing. When he got the girl to the floor, she bit his arm.

Unnecessary risk. "She won't submit to a test," Enos said after Sid's arm was washed and bandaged. Sid knew she wasn't going to submit to anything — why should she? She was upstairs in four-point restraint, doped but still raving; she was a strong girl with a shaved head, six pierced holes in one ear, a single chain looped through them all. Sid wanted Enos to define *unnecessary.*

Now he was out of harm's way. Down in Postmortem. The dead don't bite. *Unconscious men don't make choices.* Everyone pretended it was for his own sake.

Sid moved the woman from the gurney to the steel table. He was not supposed to think of her as a woman, he knew this. She was a body, female. He was not supposed to touch her thin blue hair or wrinkled eyelids — for his own sake. He was not supposed to look at her scars and imagine his mother's body — three deep puckers in one breast, a raised seam across the belly — was not supposed to see the ghost there, imprint of a son too big, taken this way, and later another scar, something else stolen while she slept. He was not to ask what they had hoped to find, opening her again.

Roxanne smoked more and more to keep from drinking. She didn't stash her cartons of cigarettes in the freezer anymore. No need. She did two packs a day, soon it would be three. Sid thought of her body, inside: her starved, black lungs shriveled in her chest, her old, swollen liver.

He knew exactly when she started again, their sixty-third day together, the thirty-ninth and final day of her sobriety.

He drew a line down her body, throat to belly, with his tongue. She didn't want to make love. She wanted to lie here, beneath the window, absolutely still. She was hot. He moved his hands along the wet, dark line he'd left on her ashy skin, as if to open her.

"Forget it," she said. The fan beat at the air, the blade of a chopper, hovering. He smelled of formaldehyde, but she didn't complain about that. It covered other smells: the garbage in the corner, her own body.

They hadn't made love for nineteen days. He had to go to his mother's tonight but was afraid to leave Roxanne naked on the bed, lighting each cigarette from the butt of the last one. He touched her hip, the sharp bone. He wanted her to know it didn't matter to him if they made love or not. If she drank or not. He didn't mind cigarette burns on the sheets, bills missing from his wallet. As long as she stayed.

The pictures of his three nieces in his mother's living room undid him. He didn't know them now, but he remembered their thin fingers, their scabbed knees, the way Lena kissed him one night — as a woman, not a child, as if she saw already how their lives would be — a solemn kiss, on the mouth, but not a lover's kiss. Twelve years old, and she must have heard her mother say, *Look, Sid, maybe it would be better if you didn't come around — just for a while — know what I mean?* When he saw her again she was fifteen and fat, seven months pregnant. Christina said, *Say hello to your uncle Sid,* and the girl stared at him, unforgiving, as if he were to blame for this too.

These were the things that broke his heart: his nieces on the piano and the piano forever out of tune; dinner served promptly at six, despite the heat; the smell of leather in the closet, a pile of rabbit skin and soft fur; the crisp white sheets of his old bed and the image of his mother bending, pulling the corners tight, tucking them down safe, a clean bed for her brave boy who was coming home.

Those sheets made him remember everything, the night sweats, the yellow stain of him on his mother's clean sheets. He washed them but she knew, and nothing was the way they expected it to be, the tossing in the too-small bed, the rust-colored blotches in his underwear, tiny slivers of shrapnel working their way to the surface, wounding him again. *How is it a man gets shot in the ass?* It was a question they never asked, and he couldn't have told them without answering other questions, questions about what had happened to the men who stepped inside the hut, who didn't have time to turn and hit the ground, who blew sky-high and fell down in pieces.

He touched his mother too often and in the wrong way. He leaned too close, tapping her arm to be sure she was listening. He tore chicken from the bone with his teeth, left his face greasy. Everything meant something it hadn't meant before.

She couldn't stand it, his big hands on her. He realized now how rarely she'd touched him. He remembered her cool palm on his forehead, pushing the hair off his face. Did he have a temperature? He couldn't remember. He felt an old slap across his mouth for a word he'd spit out once and forgotten. He remembered his mother licking her thumb and rubbing his cheek, wiping a dark smudge.

He thought of the body he couldn't touch, then or now — her velvety, loose skin over loose flesh, soft crepe folding into loose wrinkles.

His father was the one to tell him. They were outside after dinner, more than twenty years ago, but Sid could see them still, his father and himself standing at the edge of the yard by the empty hutches. Next door, Ollie Kern spoke softly to his roses in the dark. Sid could see it killed his father to do it. He cleared his throat three times before he said, "You need to find your own place to live, son." Sid nodded. He wanted to tell his father it was okay, he understood, he was ready. He wanted to say he forgave him — not just for this, but for everything, for not driving him across the border one day, to Vancouver, for not suggesting he stay there a few days, alone, for not saying, "It's okay, son, if you don't want to go."

Sid wanted to say no one should come between a husband and a wife, not even a child, but he only nodded, like a man, and his father patted his back, like a man. He said, "I guess I should turn on the sprinkler." And Sid said, "I'll do it, Dad."

They must have talked after that, many times. But in Sid's mind this was always the last time. He remembered forever crawling under the prickly juniper bushes to turn on the spigot as the last thing he did for his father. Remembered forever how they stood, silent in the dark, listening to water hitting leaves and grass.

He was in the living room now with his mother, after all these years, drinking instant coffee made from a little packet — it was all she had. It was still so hot. She said it. *It's still so hot.* It was almost dark, but they hadn't turned on the lights because of the heat, so it was easy for Sid to imagine the shadow of his father's shape in the chair, easy to believe that now might have been the time his father said at last, *Tell me, son, how it was, the truth, tell me.* It was like this. Think of the meanest boy you knew in sixth grade, the one who caught cats to cut off their tails. It's like that. But not all the time. Keep remembering your eleven-year-old self, your unbearable boy energy, how you sat in the classroom hour after hour, day after day, looking out the window at light, at rain. Remember the quivering leaves, how you felt them moving in your own body when you were a boy — it's like that, the waiting, the terrible boredom, the longing for something to happen, *anything,* so you hate the boy with the cat but you're thrilled too, and then you hate yourself, and then you hate the cat for its ridiculous howling and you're glad when it runs into the street crazy with pain — you're glad when the car hits it, smashes it flat. Then the bell rings, recess is over, and you're in the room again — you're taking your pencils out of your little wooden desk. The girl in front of you has long, shiny braids you know you'll never touch, not now, not after what you've seen, and then you imagine the braids in your hands, limp as cats' tails, and Mrs. Richards is saying the words *stifle, release, mourn,* and you're supposed to spell them, print them on the blank page, pass the paper forward, and later you're supposed to think the red marks — her sharp corrections, her grade — matter.

He could be more specific. If his father wanted to know. At night, you dig a hole in red clay and sleep in the ground. Then there's rain. Sheets and rivers and days of rain. The country turns to mud and smells of shit. A tiny cut on your toe festers and swells, opens wider and wider, oozes and stinks, an ulcer, a hole. You think about your foot all the time, more than you think about your mother, your father, minute after minute, the pain there, you care about your foot more than your life — you could lose it, your right big toe, leave it here, in this mud, your foot, your leg, and you wonder, how many pieces of yourself can you leave behind and still be called yourself? Mother, father, sister — heart, hand, leg. One mosquito's trapped under your net. You've used repellent — you're sticky with it, poisoned by it — but she finds the places you've missed: behind your ear, between your fingers. There's a sweet place up your sleeve, under your arm. And you think, *This is the wound that will kill me.* She's threading a parasite into your veins. These are the enemies: mud, rain, rot, mosquito. She's graceful. She's not malicious. She has no brain, no intentions. She wants to live, that's all. If she finds you, she'll have you. She buzzes at your head, but when she slips inside there's no sound.

It's still so hot. He wants to bang the keys of the out-of-tune piano. He wants a racket here, in his mother's house. He longs for all the dark noise of Roxanne, his plates with their tiny roses smashing to the floor two nights ago, his blue glasses flying out of the drainer. She wanted a drink, and he said she could have one, and she told him to fuck himself, and then the dishes exploded. He thinks of her walking through the broken glass, barefoot but not cutting her feet, brilliant Roxanne. *Roxanne Roxanne.* He has to say her name here, now, bring her into this room where the silent television flickers like a small fire in the corner. He wants to walk her up the stairs to that boy's room, wants her to run her fingers through the silky fur of rabbit pelts in the closet, wants to explain how fast his father was with the knife but too old, too slow, to collect tolls for the ferry. He wants to show her the tight corners of the white sheets, wants her to touch him, here, in this room, to bring him back together, who he was then, who he is now.

So he is saying it, her name. He is telling his mother, *I've been seeing someone,* and his mother is saying, *That's nice, Sid — you should bring her to dinner,* and he understands she means sometime, in some future she can't yet imagine, but he says, *Next week?*

She sips at her too-hot coffee, burns her pursed lips, says, *Fine, that would be fine.*

Roxanne will never agree to it. He knows this. He sees the glow of her cigarette moving in the dark, hand to mouth. He knows he won't ask because he can't bear the bark of her laughter. He doesn't turn on the light, doesn't speak. He sees what's happening, what will happen — this room in winter, the gray light leaking across the floor, the windows closed, the rain streaming down the glass.

He lies down beside her. She stubs out her cigarette, doesn't light another, says nothing but moves closer, so the hair of her arm brushes the hair of his.

He knows she hasn't eaten tonight, hasn't moved all day, living on cigarettes and air, a glass of orange juice he brought her hours ago. Roxanne. But she must have stood at the windows once while he was gone, he sees that now: the blinds are down; the darkness is complete, final, the heat close. There's only sound: a ship's horn on the canal; a man in the distance who wails and stops, wails and stops, turning himself into a siren. She rolls toward him, touches his lips with her tongue, presses her frail, naked body against him. He feels the bones of her back with his fingers, each disk of the spine. He knows he can't say anything — now or forever — such tender kisses, but he's afraid she'll stop, that she'll break him here, on this bed, so he holds back, in case she says she's tired or hungry, too hot, though he's shaking already, weeks of wanting her pulled into this moment. He touches her as if for the first time, each finger forming a question: *Here and here, and this way, can I?* He's trembling against his own skin, inside. If she says no, he'll shatter, break through himself, explode. She's unbuttoning his shirt, unzipping his pants, peeling him open. She's tugging his trousers down toward his feet but not off — they shackle him. And he knows if they make love this way, without talking, it will be the last time. He wants to grab her wrists and speak, but he can't — the silence is everything, hope and the lack of it. He wants the dark to come inside him, to be him, and there are no words even now, no sounds of pleasure, no soft murmurs, no names, no gods, only their skin — hot, blurred — their damp skin and the place where his becomes hers no longer clear, only her hair in his mouth, her eyes, her nose, her mouth in his mouth, her nipple, her fingers, her tongue in his mouth, brittle Roxanne going soft now, skinny Roxanne huge in the heat of them, swollen around him, her body big enough for all of him and he's down in her, all the way down in the dark and she has no edges, no outline, no place where her dark becomes the other dark, the thinning, separate air, and he doesn't know his own arms, his own legs, and still he keeps moving into her, deeper and deeper, feeling too late what she is, what she's become, softer and softer under him, the ground, the black mud, the swamp swallowing him — he's there, in that place, trying to pull himself out of it, but his boots are full of mud — he's thigh-deep, falling face down in the swamp, and then he feels fingernails digging into his back, a bony hand clutching his balls. He tries to grab her wrist but she's let go — she's slipped away from him, and he knows he never had a chance — this swamp takes everyone. He's gasping, mouth full of mud, and then there's a word, a name, a plea: *Stop, Sid, please,* and then there's a body beneath him, and then there's his body: heavy, slick with sweat, and then there's a man sitting on the edge of a mattress, his head in his hands, and then there's the air, surprising and cool, the fan beating and beating.

He opens the shades and rolls a joint, sits in the big chair, smoking. She's fallen asleep — to escape him, he thinks, and he doesn't blame her. If his father moved out of these shadows, Sid would say, Look at her. It was like this, exactly like this. After the rain, after the toe heals, after you don't die of malaria. The sniper's bullet whizzes past your ear, and you're almost relieved. You think this is an enemy you'll know. Bouncing Bettys and Toe Poppers jump out of the ground all day. Two wounded, two dead. The choppers come and take them all. You expect it to happen and it does, just after dark: one shot, and then all of you are shooting — you tear the trees apart. In the morning, you find them, two dead boys and a girl in the river. Her blood flowers around her in the muddy water. Her hands float. Her long black hair streams out around her head and moves like the river. She's the one who strung the wire, the one who made the booby trap with your grenade and a tin can. She tried to trip you up, yesterday and the day before. She's the sniper who chose you above all others. Her shot buzzed so close you thought she had you. She looks at the M-16 slung over your shoulder. She looks at your hands. She murmurs in her language which you will never understand. Then she speaks in your language. She says, Your bullet's in my liver. She tells you. Your bullet ripped my bowel. She says, Look for yourself if you don't believe me. You try to pull her from the water. You slip in the mud. The water here knows her. The mud filling your boots is her mud. Slight as she is, she could throw you down and hold you under.

How would you kill me?

You know, with my body.

But you get her to the bank. You pull her from the river. Then the medic's there and he tells you she's dead, a waste of time, *unnecessary risk,* and you tell him she wasn't dead when you got there, she wasn't, and you look at her lying on the bank, and she's not your enemy now, she's not anyone's enemy — she's just a dead girl in the grass, and you leave her there, by the river.

Sid thinks of the doctors at the hospital, their skills, how they use them, their endless exchanges — merciful, futile, extravagant — hearts and lungs, kidneys and marrow. What would they have given her, what would they have taken?

If his mother had looked out the window soon enough, if Sid had been there to carry him to the car, his father could have been saved by a valve; but the man was alone, absolutely, and the blood fluttering in his heart couldn't flow in the right direction. So he lay there in his own back yard, the hose in his hand, the water running and running in the half-dark.

Sid no longer knows when Roxanne will be lying on his bed and when she won't. She's got her own life, she tells him, and suddenly she does: friends who call at midnight, business she won't describe. One night she doesn't come home at all, but the next morning she's there, downstairs, hunched in the entryway, one eye swollen shut. *Mugged,* she says. *Son of a bitch.* And he knows what's happened. Even her cigarettes stolen. She forages for butts, checking the ashtray, the garbage. There aren't many. She's smoked them down to the filters almost every time, but she finds enough to get by while he runs to the store for a carton, for juice and bread, a jar of raspberry jam. He wants her to eat, but she won't. She doesn't give a shit about that. She doesn't give a shit about him. One line leads to the next. He nods, he knows this. She says she loves whiskey more than she loves him — the park, the tracks, the ground more than a mattress on the floor. She says the bottle's always there and sometimes he's not and who the fuck does he think he is, Jesus? And he says no, he never saved anyone. And then she's crying, beating his chest with her fists, falling limp against him, sobbing so hard he thinks her skinny body will break and he holds her until she stops and he carries her to the bed. He brings her orange juice, the jar of jam, ice in a rag for her swollen eye. She eats jam by the spoonful but no bread. He combs her tangled hair. He lays her down and she wants to make love but they don't, he can't, and he doesn't go to work that day but he does the next and then she's gone.

Days become weeks become winter, the one he imagined, the rain on the window. She's here but not here. She's left the smell of her hair on the pillow, her underpants twisted in the sheet at the foot of the bed, the butts of her cigarettes in the ashtray. He sees her everywhere. She's the boy in the hooded sweatshirt huddled on the stoop, whispering *I got what you need,* trying to sell crack or his own thin body. She's the bloated woman asleep on a bench in the park, the newspaper over her face coming apart in the rain. She's the bearded man at Pike's Market who pulls fishbones from the trash to eat the raw flesh. She's the dark man cuffed and shoved into the cruiser. She turns to stare out the back window, blaming him. She's the girl on Broadway with blond hair shaved to stubble. She's fifteen. She wears fishnets under ripped jeans, black boots, a leather jacket with studded spikes along the shoulders. She smacks gum, smokes, says *Fuck you* when he looks too long. He wants to stop, wants to warn her of the risks, wants to say, *Just go home.* But she can't, he knows; at least it's strangers on the street, not someone you know. *And anyway, what about you?* she'd say. She'd drop her cigarette, grind it out. She'd whisper, *I saw Roxanne — she's not doing too good, she's sick — so don't be giving me any shit about risk.*

She's the scarred man on the table with his twice-cleaved chest and gouged belly. When they open him, they'll find things missing. She's the woman without a name, another body from the river. He knows her. She rises, floating in the dirty water.

Dr. Juste says, "Shove her up there on the slab any way you can."

This one's fat. That's the first thing Sid notices. Later there will be other things: the downy hair on her cheeks, the long black hairs sprouting from her blotched legs, the unbelievable white expanse of her breasts. And she's dead, of course, like the others.

But she's not exactly like them, not dead so long, not so cold or stiff. He'd thought he could no longer be surprised, but she surprises him, Gloria Luby, the fattest dead person he has ever seen.

She weighs three hundred and twenty-six pounds. That gives her eighty-three on Sid and the gravity of death.

Dr. Juste turns at the door. He's lean and hard, not too tall, bald; he has a white beard, the impatience of a thin man. He says, "You'll have to roll this one." He says, "She won't mind."

Now they're alone, Gloria and Sid. She was a person a few hours ago, until the intern blasted her eyes with light and the pupils stayed frozen. Sid can't grasp it, the transformation. If she was a person in the room upstairs, she's a person still. He imagines her upstairs, alive in her bed, a mountain of a woman in white, her frizz of red hair matted and wild, no one to comb it. Blind, unblinking as a queen, she sat while the interns clustered around her and the head resident told them about her body and its defeats, the ravages of alcohol and the side effects of untreated diabetes: her engorged cirrhotic liver, the extreme edema of her abdomen, fluid accumulating from her liver disease, which accounted for her pain — were they listening to her moan? — which put pressure on her lungs till she could barely breathe — did they see her writhing under the sheets? It was the gastrointestinal bleeding that couldn't be stopped, even after the fluid was drained from the belly.

She pissed people off, getting fatter every day, filling with fluids and gases, seventeen days in all. If she'd lived two more, they would have taken her legs, which Dr. Juste says would have been a waste because it wouldn't have saved her but might have prolonged this. Sid wanted to ask what he meant, exactly, when he said *this*.

She's valuable now, at last: she's given herself up, her body in exchange for care. In an hour, Dr. Juste will begin his demonstration and Gloria Luby will be exposed, her massive mistakes revealed.

Sid thinks they owe her something, a lift instead of a shove, some trace of respect. He won't prod. He isn't going to call another orderly for help, isn't going to subject Gloria Luby to one more joke. *How many men does it take to change a light bulb for a fat lady?*

Later, he may think it isn't so important. Later, he may realize no one was watching, not even Gloria Luby. But just now this is his only duty: clear, specific. It presented itself.

None, she has to turn herself on. He knew what Juste would say when the interns gathered: *Shall we cut or blast?*

A first-timer might be sick behind his mask when they opened her abdomen and the pools of toxins began to drain into the grooves of the metal table, when the whole room filled with the smell of Gloria Luby's failures. But everyone would keep laughing, making cracks about women big enough for a man to live inside. He knew how scared they'd be, really, looking at her, the vastness of her opened body, because she *was* big enough for a man to crawl inside, like a cow, like a cave. Hollowed out, she could hide him forever. Some of them might think of this later, might dream themselves into the soft swamp of her body, might feel themselves waking in the warm, sweet, rotten smell of it, in the dark, in the slick, glistening fat with the loose bowels tangled around them. They might hear the jokes and wish to speak. Why didn't anyone notice? There's a man inside this woman, and he's alive. But he can't speak — she can't speak — the face is peeled back, the skull empty, and now the cap of bone is being plastered back in place, and now the skin is being stitched shut. The autopsy is over — she's closed, she's done — and he's still in there, with her, in another country, with the smell of shit and blood that's never going to go away, and he's not himself at all, he's her, he's Gloria Luby — bloated, full of gas, fat and white and dead forever.

It could happen to anyone. Anytime. Sid thinks, The body you hate might be your own; your worst fear might close around you, might be stitched tight by quick, clever hands. You might find yourself on this table. You might find yourself sprawled on a road or submerged in a swamp; you might find yourself in a bed upstairs, your red hair blazing, your useless legs swelling. Shadows come and go and speak, describing the deterioration of your retinas, the inefficiency of your kidneys, the necessity of amputation due to decreasing circulation in the lower extremities. *Extremities.* Your legs. They mean your legs. You might find yourself face down in your own sweet back yard, the hose still in your hand.

He doesn't think about God or ask himself what he believes — he knows: he believes in her, in Gloria Luby, in the three-hundred-and-twenty-six-pound fact of her body. He is the last person alive who will touch her with tenderness.

The others will have rubber gloves, and masks, and knives.

So he is going to lift her, gently, her whole body, not her shoulders, then her torso, then her terrible bruised thighs. She's not in pieces, not yet — she's a woman, and he is going to lift her as a woman. He is going to move her from the gurney to the table with the strength of his love.

He knows how to use his whole body, to lift from the thighs, to use the power of the back without depending on it. He crouches. It's a short lift, but he's made it harder for himself, standing between the gurney and the table. If he pressed them together, they'd almost touch — a man alone could roll her.

He squats. He works his arms under her, surprised by the coolness of her flesh, surprised, already, by her unbelievable weight.

For half a second, his faith is unwavering, and he is turning with her in his arms; they're almost there, and then something shifts — her immense left breast slaps against his chest, and something else follows; her right arm slips from his grasp — and he knows, close as they are, they'll never make it: an inch, a centimeter, a whole lifetime, lost. He feels the right knee give and twist, his own knee; he feels something deep inside tear, muscle wrenching, his knee springing out from under him, from under them. And still he holds her, trying to take the weight on the left leg, but there's no way. They hit the gurney going down, send it spinning across the room. The pain in his knee is an explosion, a booby trap, a wire across a path and hot metal ripping cartilage from bone, blasting his kneecap out his pants leg.

When they hit the floor, his leg twists behind him, and he's howling. All three hundred and twenty-six pounds of Gloria Luby pin him to the cold concrete.

She amazes him. She's rolled in his arms so his face is pressed into her soft belly. The knee is wrecked. He knows that already, doesn't need to wait for a doctor to tell him. *Destroyed.* He keeps wailing, though there's no point, no one in that room but the woman on top of him, insisting she will not hear, not ever. There's no one in the hallway, no one in the basement. There are three closed doors between Sidney Elliott and all the living.

He has to crawl out from under her, has to prod and shove at her thick flesh, has to claw at her belly to get a breath. Inch by inch he moves, dragging himself, his shattered leg, across the smooth floor. He leaves her there, just as she is, face down, the lumpy mound of her rump rising in the air.

Dr. Enos is trying not to smile while Sid explains, again, how it happened. Everyone smiles, thinking of it, Sid Elliott on the floor underneath Gloria Luby. They're sorry about his leg, truly. It's not going to be okay. There'll be a wheelchair, and then a walker. In the end, he'll get by with a cane. If he's lucky. It's a shame, Dr. Roseland tells him, to lose a leg that way, and Sid wonders if she thinks there are good ways to lose a leg. He remembers the boy on the table. He remembers all the boys. *Are those my legs?*

He's drifting in and out. He hears Roxanne laughing in the hallway. Then he sees her at the window, her mouth tight and grim as she sucks smoke.

She wants to know if it's worth it, the risk, the exchange: Gloria Luby's dignity for his leg. The *idea* of her dignity. She laughs, but it's bitter. She tells him he's a failure; she tells him how they found Gloria Luby. It took six orderlies to get her on the slab. They grunted, mocking her, cursing him.

He sleeps and wakes. Roxanne's gone. Even her smoke is gone. He asks the nurse, a thin, dark-skinned man, *Where is she? And the nurse says, Where's who, baby? Nobody been here but you and me.*

His father stands in the corner, shaking his head. He can't believe Sid's come back from the jungle, nothing worse than shrapnel in his ass, only to get it from a three-hundred-pound dead woman in a hospital in Seattle. *Three hundred and twenty-six,* Sid says. *What? Three hundred and twenty-six pounds.* His father looks as if he wants to weep, and Sid's sorry — not for himself, he'd do it again. He's sorry for his father, who's disappointed, and not just in him. He's been standing in the closet in Sid's old room all these years, sobbing in the musty dark, pressing his face into the soft rabbit fur. He's been in the other room, in the summer heat, listening to Sid plead with Roxanne, *Just let me lick you.* He's been in the kitchen, watching Sid's mother fry pork chops, chop onions, mash potatoes. He's tried to tell her something and failed. He's stood there, silent in the doorway, while she and Sid sat at the table chewing and chewing. Now, at last, when he speaks to his son, he has nothing to tell him, no wisdom to impart, only a phrase to mutter to himself, *What a waste, what a waste,* and Sid knows that when he says it he's not thinking of the leg. He wants to forgive his father for something, but the old man's turned down his hearing aid. He looks befuddled. He says, *What is it, Sid?*

The nurse shows him the button to press when the pain comes back. *Straight into the vein, babe. No need to suffer. Just give yourself a little pop. Some people think they got to be strong, lie there sweating till I remind them. Not me, honey — you give me one of those, I'd be fine all the time.* He grins. He has a wide mouth, bright teeth; he says, *You need me tonight, honey, you just buzz.*

Gloria Luby lies down beside him. She tells him, *I was exactly what they expected me to be. My brain was light, my liver heavy; the walls of my heart were thick. But there were other things they never found.* She rolls toward him, presses herself against him. Her soft body has warmth but no weight. She envelopes him. She says, *I'll tell you now, if you want to know.*

The blond girl with the spikes on her jacket leans in the doorway. Outside, the rain. Behind her, the yellow light of the hall. She's wearing her black combat boots, those ripped fishnets, a sheer black dress, a black slip. She says, *Roxanne's dead. So don't give me any of that shit about risk.* He turns to the wall. He doesn't have to listen to this. *All right then,* she says, *maybe she's not dead. But I saw her — she don't look too good.*

She comes into the room, slumps in the chair by the bed. She says, *I heard all about you and that fat lady.*

She's waiting. She thinks he'll have something to say. She lights a cigarette, says, *Wanna drag?* And he does, so they smoke, passing the cigarette back and forth. She says, *Roxanne thinks you're an idiot, but who knows.* She grinds the cigarette out on the floor, then stuffs the filter back in the pack, between the plastic and the paper. She says, *Don't tell anybody I was here.*

The nurse brings Sid a wet cloth, washes his face, says, *You been talking yourself silly, babe.*

You know what I did?

The nurse touches Sid's arm, strokes him from elbow to wrist. *You're famous here, Mr. Elliott — everybody knows what you did.*

Roxanne sits on the windowsill. She says, *Looks like you found yourself another sweetheart.*

Sid's forehead beads with sweat. The pain centers in his teeth, not his knee; it throbs through his head. He's forgotten the button on his IV, forgotten the buzzer that calls the nurse. Roxanne drifts toward the bed like smoke. She says, *Does it hurt, Sid?* He doesn't know if she's trying to be mean or trying to be kind. She says, *This is only the beginning.* But she presses the button, releases the Demerol into the tube. She stoops as if to kiss him but doesn't kiss. She whispers, *I'm gone now.*

Sidney Elliott stands in a white room at the end of a long hallway. He's alone with a woman. He looks at her. He thinks, Nobody loved you enough or in the right way.

In some part of his mind, he knows exactly what will happen if he lifts her, if he takes her home, but it's years too late to stop.

He tries to be tender.

He prays to be strong.

FATHER,

LOVER,

DEADMAN,

DREAMER

◢◢◢ I WAS a natural liar, like my mother. One night she told my daddy she was going to the movies with her girlfriend Marlene. Drive-in, double feature, up in Kalispell. Daddy said, *How late will you be?* And my mother said she didn't know.

Hours later, we tried to find her. I remember my father hobbling from car to car while I sat in the truck. The faces on the screen were as big as God's. Their voices crackled in every box. I was certain my mother was here, stunned and obedient. Huge bodies floated over the hill. They shimmered, lit from inside. This was how the dead returned, I thought, full of grace and hope.

It was midnight. I was nine years old. By morning I understood my mother was five hundred miles gone.

I remember the clumsy child I was. Bruises on my arms, scabbed knees. Boys chased me down the gully after school. I remember falling in the mud. They stole things I couldn't get back, small things whose absences I couldn't explain to my father now that we lived alone: a plastic barrette shaped like a butterfly, one shoelace, a pair of white underpants embroidered with the word *Wednesday.* I was Wednesday's child. I wore my Tuesday pants twice each week, the second day turned inside out.

Careless girl, the nuns said, immature, a dreamer. They told my father they had to smack my hands with a ruler just to wake me up.

I was afraid of the lake, the dark water, the way rocks blurred and wavered, the way they grew long necks and fins and swam below me.

I was afraid of the woods where a hunter had killed his only son. An accident, he said: the boy moved so softly in his deer-colored coat. When the man saw what he'd shot, he propped the gun between his feet and fired once more. He bled and bled. Poured into the dry ground. Unlucky man, he lived to tell.

I was afraid of my father's body, the way he was both fat and thin at the same time, like the old cows that came down to the water at dusk. Bony haunches, sagging bellies — they were pitiful things. Daddy yelled at them, waving his stick, snapping the air behind their scrawny butts. They looked at him with their terrible cow eyes. Night after night they drank all they wanted, shat where they stood. Night after night the stick became a cane, and my father climbed the path, breathing hard. He'd been a crippled child, a boy with a metal brace whose mother had had to teach him to walk a second time when he was six, a boy whose big sister lived to be ten. She drowned in air, chest paralyzed, no iron lung to save her. I thought it was this nightly failure, the cows' blank eyes, that made my mother go.

My daddy worked for a man twelve years younger than he was, a doctor with an orchard on the lake. We lived in the caretaker's cottage, a four-room cabin behind the big house. Lying in my little bed, the one Daddy'd built just for me, I heard leaves fluttering, hundreds of cherry trees; I heard water lapping stones on the shore. Kneeling at my window, I saw the moon's reflection, a silvery path rippling across the water. I smelled the pine of the boards beneath me, and the pines swaying along the road. Then, that foot-dragging sound in the hall.

I remember the creak of the hinge, my father's shape and the light behind him as he stood at my door. This was another night, years before the movie, another time my mother lied and was gone. He said, *Get dressed, Ada, we have to go.* He meant we had to look for her. He meant he couldn't leave me here alone. I wore my mother's sweater over my nightgown, the long sleeves rolled up.

This time we drove south, down through the reservation, stopping at every bar. We drove past the Church of the Good Shepherd, which stayed lit all night, past huddled trailers and tarpaper shacks, past the squat house where two dogs stood at the edge of the flat tin roof and howled, past the herd of white plaster deer that seemed to flee toward the woods.

We found my mother just across the border, beyond the reservation, in a town called Paradise, the Little Big Man Bar. Out back, the owner had seven junked cars. He called it his Indian hotel. For a buck, you could spend the night, sleep it off.

My mother was inside that bar, dancing with a dark-skinned man. Pretty Noelle, so pale she seemed to glow. She spun, head thrown back, eyes closed. She was dizzy, I was sure. The man pulled her close, whispered to make her laugh. I swear I heard that sound float, my mother's laughter weaving through the throb of guitar and drum, whirling around my head like smoke. I swear I felt that man, his hand on my own back, the shape of each finger, the sweat underneath my nightgown, underneath his palm.

Then it was my father's hand, clamping down.

I am a woman now. I have lovers. I am my mother's daughter. I dance all night. Strangers with black hair hold me close.

I remember driving home, the three of us squeezed together in the truck. I was the silence between them. I felt my father's pain in my own body, as if my left leg were withered, my bones old. Maybe I was dreaming. I saw my mother in a yellow dress. She looked very small. A door opened, far away, and she stumbled through it to a field of junked cars.

The windows in the truck were down. I was half in the dream, half out. I couldn't open my eyes, but I knew where we were by smell and sound: wood fires burning, the barking of those dogs.

I remember my prayers the morning after, boys lighting candles at the altar, my mother's white gloves.

Green curtain, priest, black box — days later I was afraid of the voice behind the screen, soft at first and then impatient, what the voice seemed to know already, what it urged me to tell. I was afraid of stained glass windows, saints and martyrs, the way sunlight fractured them, the rocks they made me want to throw.

Sometimes my father held me on his lap until I fell asleep. He stroked my hair and whispered, *So soft.* He touched my scraped shin. *What happened, Ada, did you fall down?* I nodded and closed my eyes. I thought about the boys, the gully, the things they stole. I learned that the first lie is silence. And I never told.

Then I was a girl, twelve years old, too big for my father's lap. I dove from the cliffs into the lake. I told myself the shapes waffling near the bottom were only stones.

I played a game in the woods with my friend Jean. We

shot each other with sticks and fell down in the snow. We lay side by side, not breathing. My chest felt brittle as glass. If I touched my ribs, I thought I'd splinter in the cold. The first one to move was the guilty father. The first one to speak had to beg forgiveness of the dead son.

I worked for the doctor's wife now. My mother's words hissed against those walls. I knew the shame she felt, how she hated that house, seeing it so close, getting down on her knees to wax its floors, how she thought it was wrong for an old man like my father to shovel a young man's snow.

But Daddy was glad the snow belonged to someone else. That doctor had nothing my father wanted to own. He said, *The cherry trees, they break your heart.* He meant something always went wrong: thunderstorms in July; cold wind from Canada; drought. I remember hail falling like a rain of stones, ripe fruit torn from trees. I remember brilliant sunlight after the storm, glowing ice and purple cherries splattered on the ground. My father knelt in the orchard, trying to gather the fruit that was still whole.

Then I was sixteen, almost a woman. I went to public school. I knew everything now. I refused to go to mass with my father. I said I believed in Jesus but not in God. I said if the father had seen what he'd done to his child, he would have turned the gun on himself. I thought of the nuns, my small hands, the sting of wood across my palms. I remembered their habits, rustling cloth, those sounds, murmurs above me, that false pity, *poor child*, how they judged me for what my mother had done.

I knew now why my mother had to go. How she must have despised the clump and drag of my father's steps in the hall, the weight of him at the table, the slope of his shoulders, the sorrow of his smell too close. He couldn't dance. Never drank. Old man, she said, and he was. Smoking was his only vice, Lucky Strikes, two packs a day, minus the ones I stole.

He tried not to look at me too hard. I was like her. He saw Noelle when I crossed my legs or lit my cigarette from a flame on the stove.

He gave me what I wanted — the keys to his truck, money for gas and movies, money for mascara, a down vest, a cotton blouse so light it felt like gauze. He thought if I had these things I wouldn't be tempted to steal. He thought I wouldn't envy the doctor's wife for her ruby earrings or her tiny cups rimmed with gold. Still, I took things from her, small things she didn't need: a letter opener with a silver blade and a handle carved of bone; a silk camisole; oily beads of soap that dissolved in my bathwater and smelled of lilac. I lay in the tub, dizzy with myself. The dangerous knife lay hidden, wrapped in underwear at the bottom of my drawer. Next to my skin, the ivory silk of the camisole was soft and forbidden, everything in me my father couldn't control.

The same boys who'd chased me down the gully took me and Jean to the drive-in movies in their Mustangs and Darts. Those altar boys and thieves who'd stolen my butterfly bar-rette pleaded with me now: *Just once, Ada — I promise I won't tell.*

I heard Jean in the back seat, going too far.

Afterward, I held her tight and rocked. Her skin smelled of sweet wine. I said, *You'll be okay. I promise, you will.*

I am a woman now, remembering. I live in a trailer, smaller than my father's cottage. I am his daughter after all: there's nothing I want to own. I drive an old Ford. I keep a pint of whiskey in the glovebox, two nips of tequila in my purse. I don't think I know as much as I used to know. I sit in the car with my lights off and watch my father, the slow shape of him swimming through the murky light of his little house. He's no longer fat and thin. It scares me, the way he is thin alone. He's had two heart attacks. His gallbladder and one testicle are gone. In January, the doctors in Spokane opened his chest to take pieces of his lungs. Still he smokes. He's seventy-six. He says, *Why stop now?*

I smoke too, watching him. I drink. I tell myself I'm too drunk to knock at the door, too drunk to drive home.

In the grass behind my father's cottage, a green truck sits without tires, sinking into the ground. If I close my eyes and touch its fender, I can feel everything: each shard, the headlight shattering, the stained glass windows bursting at last, the white feet of all the saints splintering, slicing through a man's clothes.

Twenty-one years since that night, but if I lie down beside that truck, I can feel every stone of a black road.

Fourth of July, 1971. This is how the night began, with my small lies, with tepid bathwater and the smell of lilac — with ivory silk under ivory gauze — with the letter opener slipped in my purse. I was thinking of the gully long before, believing I was big enough to protect myself.

Jean and I knew other boys now. Boys who crashed parties in the borderlands at the edge of every town.

I asked my father for the truck. I promised: *Jean's house, then up the lake to Bigfork to see the fireworks and nowhere else.* I said, *Yes, straight home.* I twisted my hair around my finger, remembering my mother in a yellow dress, lying to my father and me, standing just like this, all her weight on one foot, leaning against the frame of this door.

We drove south instead of north. A week before, two boys in a parking lot had offered rum and let us sit in the back seat of their car. They said, *Come to the reservation if you want to see real fireworks.*

We scrambled down a gulch to a pond. Dusk already and there were maybe forty kids at the shore.

We were white girls, the only ones.

Jean had three six-packs, two to drink and one to share. I had a pint of vodka and a quart of orange juice, a jar to shake them up. But the Indian kids were drinking pink gasoline — Hawaiian Punch and ethanol — chasing it down with bottles of Thunderbird. They had boxes full of firecrackers, home-made rockets and shooting stars. They had crazyhorses that streaked across the sky. Crazy, they said, because they fooled you every time: you never knew where they were going to go.

The sky sparked. Stars fell into the pond and sizzled out. We looked for the boys, the ones who'd invited us, but there were too many dressed the same, in blue jeans and plaid shirts, too many cowboy hats pulled down.

One boy hung on to a torch until his whole body glowed. I saw white teeth, slash of red shirt, denim jacket open down the front. I thought, *He wants to burn.* But he whooped, tossed the flare in time. It spiraled toward the pond, shooting flames back into the boxes up the shore. Firecrackers popped like guns; red comets soared; crazyhorses zigzagged along the beach, across the water, into the crowd.

The boy was gone.

In the blasts of light, I saw fragments of bodies, scorched earth, people running up the hill, people falling, arms and legs in the flickering grass, one hand raised, three heads rolling, and then the strangest noise: giggles rippling, a chorus of girls.

They called to the boy, their voices like their laughter, a thin, fluttery sound. *Niles.* They sang his name across the water.

Then I was lying in the grass with that boy. Cold stars swirled in the hole of the sky. In the weird silence, bodies mended; bodies became shape and shadow; pieces were found. Flame became pink gasoline guzzled down. Gunfire turned to curse and moan.

This boy was the only one I wanted, the brave one, the crazy one, the one who blazed out. He rose up from the water, red shirt soaked, jacket torn off. I said, *You were something,* and he sat down. Now I was wet too, my clothes and hair dripping, as if he'd taken me into the sky, as if we'd both fallen into the pond.

I whispered his name, *Niles,* hummed it like the girls, but soft. He said, *Call me Yellow Dog.*

My purse was gone, the letter opener and my keys lost. The boy kept drinking that pink gasoline and I wondered how he'd die, if he'd go blind on ethanol or catch fire and drown. I'd heard stories my whole life. The Indians were always killing themselves: leaping off bridges, inhaling ammonia, stepping in front of trucks. Barefoot girls with bruised faces wandered into the snow and lay down till the snow melted around them, till it froze hard.

But tonight this boy was strong.

Tonight this boy could not be killed by gas or flame or gun.

He had a stone in his pocket, small and smooth, like a bird's egg and almost blue. He let me touch it. He said it got heavy sometimes. He said, *That's when I watch my back — that's how I know.* I kissed him. I put my tongue deep in his mouth. I said, *How much does it weigh now?* And he said, *Baby, it's dragging me down.*

My clothes dried stiff with mud. I remember grabbing his coarse braid, how it seemed alive, how I wanted it for myself. I thought I'd snip it off when he passed out. His hands were down my cut-off jeans. He knew my thoughts exactly. He whispered, *I'll slit your throat.* I let his long hair go. His body on me was heavy now. I thought he must be afraid. I thought it must be the stone. He held me down in the dirt, pressed hard: he wanted to stop my breath; he wanted to squeeze the blood from my heart. I clutched his wrists. I said, *Enough.*

I imagined my father pacing the house, that sound in the hall. I heard my own lies spit back at me, felt them twist around bare skin, a burning rope.

I remember ramming my knee into the boy's crotch, his yelp and curse, me rolling free. I called to Jean, heard her blurred answer rise out of some distant ground.

I remember crawling, scraping my knees, feeling for my purse in the grass. Then he was on me, tugging at my un-zipped jeans, wrenching my arm. He said, *I could break every bone.* But he didn't. He stood up, this Niles, this Yellow Dog. He said, *Go home.*

He was the one to find my purse. He took the letter opener, licked the silver blade, slid it under his belt. He dropped my keys beside me. He said, *I could have thrown these in the water.* He said, *I didn't. You know why? Because I want your white ass gone.*

When I looked up, the stars above him spun.

I yelled Jean's name again. I said, *Are you okay?* And she said, *Fuck you — go.*

I staggered up the hill. I saw my father at the kitchen table, his head in his hands. I heard every word of his prayers as if I were some terrible god. I felt that tightness in my chest, his body. I felt my left leg giving out.

I saw what he saw, my mother's yellow dress, me standing in the door. I smelled his cigarettes. He said, *The cherry trees, they break your heart.*

I drove up that road through the reservation, my mother's laughter floating through the open windows of the truck. She made me dizzy, all that dancing — I felt myself pulled forward, twirled, pushed back, hard.

The lights of the steeple still burned. I was Noelle, the same kind of woman, a girl who couldn't stand up by herself. I wanted to weep for my father. I wanted not to be drunk when I got home, not to smell of boy's sweat, sulfur and crushed lilacs, mud. I wanted to stop feeling hair between my fingers, to stop feeling hands slipping under my clothes.

The dogs on the roof growled. All the white plaster deer surged toward the road. Wind on my face blew cold.

Past the Church of the Good Shepherd, a hundred pairs of eyes watched from the woods, all the living deer hidden between trees along this road. I practiced lies to tell when I got home. I thought, My mother and I, we're blood and bone. I saw how every lie would be undone. I watched a dark man wrap his arms around my pale mother and spin her into a funnel of smoke.

Then he was there, that very man, rising up in a swirl of dust at the side of the road — a vision, a ghost, weaving in front of me. Then he was real, a body in dark clothes.

There was no time for a drunken girl to stop.

No time to lift my heavy foot from the gas.

I saw his body fly, then fall.

I saw the thickness of it, as if for a moment the whole night gathered in one place to become that man, my mother's lover. A door opened at the back of a bar in Paradise. His body filled that space, so black even the stars went out.

I am a woman now, remembering. I am a woman drinking whiskey in a cold car, watching the lights in my father's house. I am a woman who wants to open his door in time, to find her father there and tell.

Twenty-one years since I met Vincent Blew on that road, twenty-one years, and I swear, even now, when I touch my bare skin, when I smell lilacs, I can feel him, how warm he was, how his skin became my shadow, how I wear it still.

He was just another drunken Indian trying to find his way home. After he met me, he hid his body in the tall grass all night and the next day. Almost dusk before he was found. There was time for a smashed headlight to be reassembled. Time for a dented fender to be pounded out and dabbed with fresh green paint. Time for a girl to sober up. Time for lies to be retold. Here, behind my father's cottage, I can feel the body of the truck, that fender, the edges of the paint, how it chipped and peeled, how the cracks filled with rust.

I waited for two men in boots and mirrored glasses to come for me, to take me to a room, close the door, to ask me questions in voices too low for my father to hear, to urge and probe, to promise no one would hurt me if I simply told the truth.

Imagine: *No hurt.*

But no one asked.

And no one told.

I wanted them to come. I thought their questions would feel like love, that relentless desire to know.

I waited for them.

I'm waiting now.

I know the man on the road that night was not my mother's lover. He was Vincent Blew. He was mine alone.

He lies down beside me in my narrow bed. I think it is the bed my father built. The smell of pine breaks my heart. He touches me in my sleep, traces the cage of my ribs. He says, *You remind me of somebody.* He wets one finger and carves a line down the center of my body, throat to crotch. He says, *This is the line only I can cross.* He lays his head in the hollow of my pelvis. He says, *Yes, I remember you, every bone.*

He was behind me now, already lost.

I didn't decide anything. I just drove. My hands were wet. Blood poured from my nose. I'd struck the steering wheel. I was hurt, but too numb to know. Then I was sobbing in my father's arms. He was saying, *Ada, stop.*

Finally I choked it out.

I said, *I hit something on the road.*

And he said, *A deer?*

This lie came so easily.

All I had to do was nod.

He wrapped me in a wool blanket. Still I shivered, quick spasms, a coldness I'd never known, like falling through the ice of a pond and lying on the bottom, watching the water close above you, freeze hard. He washed the blood from my face with a warm cloth. His tenderness killed me, the way he was so careful, the way he looked at the bruises and the blood but not at me. Every gesture promised I'd never have to tell. He said, *You'll have black eyes, but I don't think your nose is broken.* These words — he meant to comfort me — precious nose — as if my own face, the way it looked, could matter now.

He said he had to check the truck. He took his flashlight, hobbled out. I couldn't stand it, the waiting — even those minutes. I thought, My whole future, the rest of my life, like this, impossibly long.

I moved to the window to watch. I tried to light a cigarette, but the match kept hissing out. I saw the beam moving over the fender and grille, my father's hand touching the truck. I imagined what he felt — a man's hair and bones. I believed he'd come back inside and sit beside me, both of us so still. If he touched me, I'd break and tell.

But when he came inside, he didn't sit, didn't ask what, only where. I could have lied again, named a place between these orchards and Bigfork, that safe road, but I believed my father was offering me a chance, this last one. I thought the truth might save us even now. I described the place exactly, the curve, the line of trees, the funnel of dust. But I did not say one thing, did not tell him, *Look for a man in the grass.*

He said, *You sleep now.* He said, *Don't answer the phone.*

I had this crazy hope. I'd heard stories of men who slammed into trees, men so drunk their bodies went limp as their cars were crushed. Some walked away. Some sailed off bridges but bobbed to the surface face up. I remembered the man's grace when we collided, the strange elegance of his limbs as he flew.

I believed in my father, those hands holding blossoms in spring, those fingers touching the fender, my face — those hands wringing the rag, my blood, into the sink. I believed in small miracles, Niles flying into the pond hours ago, Yellow Dog wading out.

I imagined my crippled father helping the dazed man stumble to the truck, driving him to the hospital for x-rays or just taking him home. I thought my father had gone back alone so that he could lift the burden of my crime from me and carry it himself, to teach me suffering and sacrifice, the mercy of his God.

Even if the police came, they'd blame the Indian himself. He'd reel, still drunk, while my father, my good father, stood sober as a nun.

For almost an hour I told myself these lies. Confession would be a private thing, to my father, no one else. He would decide my penance. I would lie down on any floor. I would ask the Holy Mother to show me how I might atone. I would forgive the priest his ignorance when wine turned to blood in my mouth.

I thought of the cherries my father found after the hail, the bowl of them he brought back to the cottage — I thought of this small miracle, that any had been left whole. We ate them without speaking, as if they were the only food. I saw my father on his knees again, the highway. He gathered all the pieces. Glass and stone became the body of a man. My father's fingers pressed the neck and found the pulse. I knew I couldn't live through fifteen minutes if what I believed was not so.

Two hours gone. I saw the bowl slipping from my hands, my faith shattered, cherries rolling across the floor. I saw the man more clearly than I had on the road, the impossible angles of his body, how he must have broken when he fell.

I heard my father say, *Thou shalt not kill.*

But this was not my crime. The Indian himself told me he accepted accidents, my drunkenness as well as his own. Then he whispered, *But I don't understand why you left me here alone.*

I knew I should have gone with my father, to show him the way. I imagined him limping up and down that stretch of highway, waving his flashlight, calling out. On this road, wind had shape and leaves spoke. A bobcat's eyes flashed. A coyote crossed the road. I felt how tired my father must be, that old pain throbbing deep in the bone.

I tried not to count all the minutes till dawn. I tried to live in this minute alone. I wanted to speak to the man, to tell him he had to live like me, like this, one minute to the next. I knew the night was too long to imagine while his blood was spilling out. I promised, *He'll come.* I said, *Just stay with your body that long. There's a hospital down the road where they have bags of blood to hang above your bed, blood to flow through tubes and needles into your veins — enough blood to fill your body again and again.*

I went to the bathroom, turned on the heater. I needed this, the smallest room, the closed door. I crushed the beads of lilac soap till I was sick with the smell. I heard the last crickets and the first birds, and I thought, *No, not yet.* I heard the man say, *I'm still breathing but not for long.* He told me, *Once I sold three pints of blood in two days.* He said, *I could use some of that back now.*

Then there were edges of light at the window and the phone was ringing. Jean's mother, I thought. I saw my friend naked, passed out in the dirt or drowned in the pond. This too my fault.

The phone again. The police at last.

I must have closed my eyes, relieved, imagining questions and handcuffs, a fast car, a safe cell. Soon, so soon, I wouldn't be alone.

I must have dreamed.

The phone kept ringing.

This time I picked it up.

It was the Indian boy. He said, *I'll slit your throat.*

Past noon before my father got home. I understood exactly what he'd done as soon as I saw the truck: the fender was undented, the headlight magically whole. I knew he must have gone all the way to Missoula, to a garage where men with greasy fingers asked no questions, where a man's cash could buy a girl's freedom.

I couldn't believe this was his choice. Couldn't believe that this small thing, the mockery of metal and glass, my crime erased, was the only miracle he could trust.

He said, *Did you sleep?* I shook my head. He said, *Well, you should.*

I thought, How can he speak to me this way if he knows what I've done? Then I thought, We, not I — it's both of us now.

The phone once more. I picked it up before he could say *Stop.* The police, I hoped. They'll save me since my father won't. But it was Jean. *Thanks a lot,* she said. *I'm grounded for a month.*

Then she hung up.

Vincent Blew was long dead when he was found. The headline said, UNIDENTIFIED MAN VICTIM OF HIT AND RUN. One paragraph. Enough words to reveal how insignificant his life was. Enough words to lay the proper blame: "elevated blood alcohol level indicates native man was highly intoxicated."

I thought, Yes, we will each answer for our own deaths.

Then there were these words, meant to comfort the killer, I suppose: "Injuries suggest he died on impact."

I knew what people would think, reading this. Just one Indian killing another on a reservation road. Let the tribal police figure it out.

Still, the newspaper gave me a kind of hope. I found it folded on the kitchen table, beside my father's empty mug. I thought, He believed my lie about the deer until today. He is that good. He fixed the truck so the doctor wouldn't see. He was ashamed of my drunkenness, that's all.

I was calm.

When he comes home, we'll sit at this table. He'll ask nothing. Father of infinite patience. He'll wait for me to tell it all. When I stop speaking, we'll drive to town. He'll stay beside me. But he won't hang on.

I was so grateful I had to lean against the wall to keep from falling down.

I thought, He loves me this much, to listen, to go with me, to give me up.

All these years I'd been wrong about the hunter. Now I saw the father's grief, how he suffered with his wounds, how his passion surpassed the dead son's. I saw the boy's deception, that deer-colored coat. I understood it was the child's silent stupidity that made the father turn the gun on himself.

I meant to say this as well.

But my father stayed in the orchard all day. At four, I put on dark glasses and went to the doctor's house. I polished gold faucets and the copper bottoms of pots; I got down on my hands and knees to scrub each tile of the bathroom floor. The doctor's wife stood in the doorway, watching me from behind.

She said, *That's nice, Ada.*

She said, *Don't forget the tub.*

When I came back to the cottage, I saw the paper stuffed in the trash, the mug washed. My father asked what I wanted for dinner, and I told him I was going to town. He said I could use the truck, and I said, *I know.*

I meant I knew there was nothing he'd refuse.

He saw me held tight in the dead Indian's arms. He was afraid of me, the truth I could tell.

Sometimes when I dream, the night I met Vincent Blew is just a movie I'm watching. Every body is huge. Yellow Dog's brilliant face fills the screen. He grins. He hangs on to that torch too long. I try to close my eyes, but the lids won't come down. His body bursts, shards of light; his body tears the sky apart. Then everything's on fire: pond, grass, hair — boy's breath, red shirt.

But later he's alive. He's an angel rising above me. He's Vincent Blew hovering over the road. The truck passes through him, no resistance, no jolt — no girl with black eyes, no body in the grass, no bloody nose. There's a whisper instead, a ragged voice full of static coming up from the ground. It's Vincent murmuring just to me: *You're drunk, little girl. Close your eyes. I'll steer. I'll get us home.*

And these nights, when he takes the wheel, when he saves us, these nights are the worst of all.

Three days before the man was known. His cousin claimed him. She said she danced with him the night he died. In Ronan, at the Wild Horse Bar. Then he was Vincent Blew, and she was Simone Falling Bear. It amazed me to think of it, the dead man dancing, the dead man in another woman's arms.

She said he died just a mile from her house. I knew then that her cousin Vincent was her lover too, that her house was a tarpaper shack at the end of a dirt road, that her refrigerator was a box of ice, her heater a woodstove. She'd have a bag of potatoes in a pail under the sink, a stack of cans with no labels on the shelf.

I saw that even in his stupor Vincent Blew knew the way home.

She said he'd been an altar boy, that he knew the words of the Latin mass by heart. She said he'd saved two men at Ia Drang and maybe more. She had his Medal of Honor as proof.

She said he wanted to open a school on the reservation where the children would learn to speak in their own tongue.

But that was before the war, before he started to drink so much.

He had these dreams. He had a Purple Heart. *Look at his chest. They had to staple his bones shut.*

I don't know what lies the reporter told to make Simone Falling Bear talk. Perhaps he said, *We want people to understand your loss.*

That reporter found Vincent's wife in Yakima, living with another man. He asked her about Vietnam, and she said she never saw any medals. She said Vincent's school was just some crazy talk, and that boy was drinking beer from his mama's bottle when he was three years old. When the reporter asked if Vincent Blew was ever a Catholic, she laughed. She said, *Everybody was.*

In a dream I climb a hill to find Vincent's mother. She lives in a cave, behind rocks. I have to move a stone to get her out. She points to three sticks stuck in the dirt. She says, *This is my daughter; these are my sons.*

September, and Vincent Blew was two months dead. I was supposed to go to school, ride the bus, drink milk. But I couldn't be with those children. Couldn't raise my hand or sit in the cafeteria and eat my lunch. I went to the lake instead, swam in the cold water till my chest hurt and my arms went numb. Fallen trees lay just below the surface; rocks lay deeper still. I knew what they were. I wasn't afraid. Only my own shadow moved.

I came home at the usual time to make dinner for my father. Fried chicken, green beans. I remember snapping each one. He didn't ask, *How was school?* I thought he knew, again, and didn't want to know, didn't want to risk the question, any question — my weeping, the truth sputtered out at last, those words so close: *Daddy, I can't.*

The next day I lay on the beach for hours. I burned. My clothes hurt my skin. I thought, He'll see this.

But again we ate our dinner in silence, only the clink of silverware, the strain of swallowing, his muttered *Thank you* when I cleared his plate. He sat on the porch while I washed the dishes, didn't come back inside till he heard the safe click, my bedroom door closed.

I saw how it was between us now. He hated each sound: the match striking, my breath sucked back, the weight of me on the floor. He knew exactly where I was — every moment — by the creak of loose boards. I learned how words stung, even the most harmless ones: *Rice tonight, or potatoes?* He had to look away to answer. *Rice, please.*

His childhood wounds, his sister's death — those sorrows couldn't touch his faith. My mother, with all her lies, couldn't break him. Only his daughter could do that. I was the occasion of sin. I was the road and the truck he was driving. He couldn't turn back.

The third day, he said, *They called from school.*

I nodded. *I'll go,* I said.

He nodded too, and that was the end of it.

But I didn't go. I hitched to Kalispell, went to six restaurants, finally found a job at a truck stop west of town.

That night I told my father I needed the truck to get to work, eleven to seven, graveyard.

I knew he wouldn't speak enough words to argue.

I married the first trucker who asked. I was eighteen. It didn't last. He had a wife in Ellensburg already, five kids. After that I rented a room in Kalispell, a safe place with high, tiny windows. Even the most careless girl couldn't fall.

Then it was March, the year I was twenty, and my father had his first heart attack. I quit my job and tried to go home. I thought he'd let me take care of him, that I could bear the silence between us.

Three weeks I slept in my father's house, my old room, the little bed.

One morning I slept too long. Light filled the window, flooded across the floor. It terrified me, how bright it was.

I felt my father gone.

In his room, I saw the bed neatly made, covers pulled tight, corners tucked.

I found him outside the doctor's house. He had his gun in one hand, the hose in the other. He'd flushed three rats from under the porch and shot them all.

He meant he could take care of himself.

He meant he wanted me to go.

I got a day job, south of Ronan this time, the Morning After Café. Seventeen years I've stayed. I live in a trailer not so many miles from the dirt road that leads to Simone Falling Bear's shack.

Sometimes I see her in the bars — Buffalo Bill's, Wild Horse, Lucy's Chance. She recognizes me, a regular, like herself. She tips her beer, masking her face in a flash of green glass.

When she stares, I think, She sees me for who I really am. But then I realize she's staring at the air, a place between us, and I think, Yes, if we both stare at the same place at the same time, we'll see him there. But she looks at the bottle again, her loose change on the bar, her own two hands.

Tonight I didn't see Simone. Tonight I danced. Once I was a pretty girl. Like Noelle, shining in her pale skin. It's not vain to say I was like that. I'm thirty-seven now, already old. Some women go to loose flesh, some to hard bone. I'm all edges from years living on whiskey and smoke.

But I can still fool men in these dim bars. I can fix myself up, curl my hair, paint my mouth. I have a beautiful blue dress, a bra with wires in the cups. I dance all night. I spin like Noelle; I shine, all sweat and blush and will.

Hours later, in my trailer, it doesn't matter, it's too late. The stranger I'm with doesn't care how I look: he only wants me to keep moving in the dark.

Drifters, liars — men who don't ask questions, men with tattoos and scars, men just busted out, men on parole; men with guns in their pockets, secrets of their own; men who can't love me, who don't pretend, who never want to stay too long: these men leave spaces, nights between that Vincent fills. He opens me. I'm the ground. Dirt and stone. He digs at me with both hands. He wants to lie down.

Or it's the other way around. It's winter. It's cold. I'm alone in the woods with my father's gun. I'll freeze. I'll starve. I look for rabbits, pray for deer. I try to cut a hole in the frozen earth, but it's too hard.

It's a bear I have to kill, a body I have to open if I want to stay warm. I have to live in him forever, hidden in his fur, down deep in the smell of bear stomach and bear heart. We lumber through the woods like this. I've lost my human voice. Nobody but the bear understands me now.

Last week my lover was a white man with black stripes tattooed across his back. His left arm was withered. *Useless,* he told me. *Shrapnel, Dak To.*

He was a small man, thin, but heavier than you'd expect.

He had a smooth stone in his pocket, three dollars in his hatband, the queen of spades in his boot. He said, *She brings me luck.*

He showed me the jagged purple scar above one kidney, told the story of a knife that couldn't kill.

The week before, my lover was bald and pale, his fingers thick. He spoke Latin in his sleep; he touched my mouth.

It's always like this. It's always Vincent coming to me through them.

This bald one said he loaded wounded men into helicopters, medevacs in Song Be and Dalat. Sometimes he rode with them. One time all of them were dead.

He was inside me when he told me that.

He robbed a convenience store in Seattle, a liquor store in Spokane. He did time in Walla Walla. I heard his switchblade spring and click. Felt it at my throat before I saw it flash.

He said, *They say I killed a man.*

He said, *But I saved more than that.*

He had two daughters, a wife somewhere. They didn't want him back.

The cool knife still pressed my neck. He said, *I'm innocent.*

I have nothing to lose. Nothing precious for a lover to steal — no ruby earrings, no silver candlesticks.

In my refrigerator he'll find Tabasco sauce and mayonnaise, six eggs, a dozen beers.

In my freezer, vodka, a bottle so cold it burns your hands.

In my cupboard, salted peanuts, crackers shaped like little fish, a jar of sugar, an empty tin.

In my closet, the blue dress that fooled him.

If my lover is lucky, maybe I'll still have yesterday's tips.

When he kisses me on the steps, I'll know that's my thirty-four dollars bulging in his pocket. I'll know I won't see him again.

He never takes the keys to my car. It's old, too easily trapped.

But tonight I have no lover. Tonight I danced in Paradise with a black-haired man. I clutched his coarse braid. All these years and I still wanted it. He pulled me close so I could feel the knife in his pocket. He said, *Remember, I have this.*

I don't know if he said the words out loud or if they were in my head.

When I closed my eyes I thought he could be that boy, the one who blew himself into the sky, whose body fell down in pieces thin and white as ash and bread, the one who rose up whole and dripping, who slipped his tongue in my mouth, his hands down my pants.

He could have been that boy grown to a man.

But when I opened my eyes I thought, No, that boy is dead.

Later we were laughing, licking salt, shooting tequila. We kissed, our mouths sour with lime. He said we could go out back. He said if I had a dollar he'd pay the man. I gave him five, and he said we could stay the week for that. I kissed him one more time, light and quick. I said I had to use the ladies' room.

Lady? he said, and he laughed.

I decided then. He was that boy, just like him. I said, *Sit tight, baby, I'll be right back.* He put his hand on my hip. *Don't make me wait,* he said.

I stepped outside, took my car, drove fast.

Don't get me wrong.

I'm not too good for Niles Yellow Dog or any man. I'm

not too clean to spend the night at that hotel. It wouldn't be the first time I passed out on a back seat somewhere, hot and drunk under someone's shadow, wrapped tight in a man's brown skin.

But tonight I couldn't do it. Tonight I came here, to my father's house, instead. Tonight I watch him.

He's stopped moving now. He's in the chair. There's one light on, above his head. I can't help myself: I drink the whiskey I keep stashed. It stings my lips and throat, burns inside my chest. But even this can't last.

I don't believe in forgiveness for some crimes. I don't believe confessions to God can save the soul or raise the dead. Some bodies are never whole again.

I cannot open the veins of my father's heart.

I cannot heal his lungs or mend his bones.

Tonight I believe only this: we should have gone back. We should have crawled through the grass until we found that man.

If Vincent Blew had one more breath, I should have lain down beside him — so he wouldn't be cold, so he wouldn't be scared.

If Vincent Blew was dead, we should have dug the hard ground with our bare hands. I should have become the dirt if he asked. Then my father could have walked away, free of my burden, carrying only his own heart and the memory of our bones, a small bag of sticks light enough to lift with one hand.

LITTLE WHITE SISTER

/// MAMA WARNED ME, stay away from white girls. Once I didn't. So, thirty years too late, I'm minding my mama. That's how it happened.

I saw her. Flurries that night and she's running, bare-legged, wearing almost nothing at all, and the snow's rising up in funnels, like ghosts, spinning across the street till they whip themselves against the bricks, and I'm thinking, Crazy white girl don't know enough to come in from the cold.

Crackhead most likely, not feeling the wind. I'd seen the abandoned car at the end of the block, ten days now, shooting gallery on wheels, going nowhere. One of them, I told myself, pissed at her boyfriend or so high she thinks her skin is burning off her. Most times crackheads don't know where they are. Like last week. Girl comes pounding on my door. White girl. Could've been the same one. Says she's looking for Lenny. Says she was here with him last night. And I say, *Lenny ain't here*, and she says, *Let me in*. I don't like arguing with a white girl in my hallway, so I let her in. I say, *Look around*. She says, *Shit — this isn't even the right place*. She says, *What're you tryin' to pull here, buddy?* And I back away, I say, *Get out of here*. I say, *I don't want no trouble*, and she says, *Damn straight you don't want no trouble*. Then she's gone but I'm thinking, You can be in it that fast and it's nothing you did, it's just something that happens.

See, I've already done my time. Walpole, nine years. And I'm not saying Rita's the only reason I went down, but I'm telling you, the time wouldn't have been so hard if not for the white girl.

Cold turkey in a cage and I know Rita's in a clinic, sipping methadone and orange juice. I'm on the floor, my whole body twisted, trying to strangle itself — bowels wrung like rags, squeezed dry, ribs clamped down on lungs so I can't breathe, my heart a fist, beating itself. And I think I'm screaming; I must be screaming, and my skin's on fire, but nobody comes, and nobody brings water, and I want to be dead and out of my skin.

Then I'm cold, shaking so hard I think my bones will break, and that's when the rabbitman slips in between the bars. The rabbitman says, *Once an axe flew off its handle, split an over-seer's skull, cleaved it clean, and I saw how easily the body opens, how gladly gives itself up; I saw how the coil of a man's brains spills from his head — even as his mouth opens, even as he tries to speak. Then I saw a blue shadow of a man — people say he ran so fast he ran out of his own skin and they never found him, the rabbitman, but I tell you, they took my skin and I was still alive.* Then the rabbitman whispered, *I got news for you, little brother. I been talkin' to the man and he told me, it ain't time yet for this nigger to die.*

So no, I don't go chasing that girl in the street. I know she'll be cold fast, but I think, Not my business — let one of her friends find her.

See, since Rita, I don't have much sympathy for white girls. And I'm remembering what my mama told me, and I'm re-membering the picture of that boy they pulled out of the Tallahatchie, sweet smiling boy like I was then, fourteen years

old and a white girl's picture in his wallet, so he don't think
nothing of being friendly with a white woman in a store. Then
the other picture — skull crushed, eye gouged out, only the
ring on his finger to tell his mama who he was, everything else
that was his boy's life gone: cocky grin, sleepy eyes, felt hat,
his skinny-hipped way of walking, all that gone, dragged to the
bottom of the river by a cotton-gin fan tied to his neck with
barbed wire. Mama said she wasn't trying to turn me mean but
she wanted me to see — for my own good, because she loved
me, which is why she did everything, because she'd die if
anything happened to me — and I thought even then something was bound to happen sooner or later, the fact of living in
my black skin a crime I couldn't possibly escape. I only had to
look once for one second to carry him around with me the rest
of my life, like a photograph in my back pocket that didn't
crack or fade, that just got sharper instead, clear as glass and
just as dangerous till I pulled it out one day and realized I'd
been staring at myself all those years.

I thought about that boy when I met Rita. He breathed on
my neck and I laughed to make him stop. I didn't go after her.
It was nothing like that. It was just something that happened,
like the white girl pounding at my door — I was watching it,
then I was in it.

We were at Wally's, me and Leo Stokes, listening to the
music, jazz — we liked the music. Mostly I'm listening to the
drummer, thinking he don't got it right. He thinks he's too
important. He don't know the drums are supposed to be the
sound underneath the sound. That's why I'm good, that's why
I want to play — I got a gift. I hear a sound below horn and
piano, the one they need, like I did back in Virginia living in
one room — Mama and Daddy, Bernice and Leroy and me,

and there were lots of sounds all the time, but I'm always listening for the one sound, like at night when Mama and Daddy are fighting and her voice keeps climbing higher and higher like it's gonna break, and his is low and hard and slow, and then they're tangled together and the words don't make sense, but I'm not scared, no matter how bad it gets, because I'm listening. I hear a whippoorwill or grasshoppers, the wings of cicadas in July, a frenzy of wings rubbing, trying to wear themselves down, and I know what they want — I know what we all want — and it's like that sound is holding everything else together, so even if Mama starts crying, and even if Daddy leaves and don't come back till afternoon the next day, and even if they stop arguing and the other sounds start, even if Daddy has to put his hand over Mama's mouth and say, *Hush now, the children,* even if they get so quiet I can't hear their breathing, I know everything's okay and I'm safe, because the cicadas are out there, and they've been there all along, even when I didn't know I was hearing them — that one sound's been steady, that one sound's been holding everything tight. So I'm listening to the music, thinking, This drummer don't know his place. He thinks he's got to get on top of things. And I hear Leo say, *Luck or trouble, little brother, heading this way,* and then she's there, standing too close, standing above me. She's saying, *Spare a cigarette?* She's whispering, *Got a light?* And then she's sitting down with us and she's got her hand on my hand while I light her cigarette and I'm thinking she's pretty — in a way, in this light — and she's older, so I think she knows things — and I ask myself what's the harm of letting her sit here, and that's when I laugh to make the boy's breath and my mama's voice go away.

Then later that night I'm looking at my own dark hand on

her thin white neck and it scares me, the difference, the color of me, the size, and she says, *What color is the inside of your mouth, the inside of your chest?* She says, *Open me — do I bleed, do my bones break?* She says, *Kiss me, we're the same.* And I do. And we are. When we're alone, we are.

She came to see me once. Cried, said she was sorry, and I sat there looking like I had stones in my stomach, ashes in my chest, like I didn't want to put my hands around her neck to touch that damp place under her hair. I told myself, She's not so pretty anymore. She looked old. The way white women do. Too skinny. Cigarettes and sun making her skin crack. Purple marks dark as bruises under her green eyes. I said, *Look, baby, I'm tired, you get on home.* I'm acting like I can't wait to get back to my cell, like I'm looking forward to the next three thousand nights smelling nothing but my own rotten self, like I've got some desire to spend nine years looking at the bodies of men, like I haven't already wondered how long it's gonna be before I want them. She says she didn't know, she didn't mean to make it worse for me, and I say, *Where you been living, girl? What country?* She's not crying then, she's pissed. She says, *You know what they did to me when I came in here? You know where they touched me?* And I say, *One day. One friggin' hour of your life. I live here, baby. They touch me all the time. Whenever they want. Wherever.*

I'm not saying she stuck the needle in my arm and turned me into a thief. I'm saying I wasn't alone. Plenty of things I did I shouldn't have. I paid for those. Three burglaries, nine years, you figure. So yeah, I paid for a dozen crimes they never slapped on me, a hundred petty thefts. But the man don't mind about your grandfather's gold pocket watch; he don't worry when the ten-dollar bill flies out of your mama's purse and floats into your hand. He don't bother you much if he sees you shoving weed on your own street. But that was different. Back when I was peddling for Leo I had a purpose, doing what I had to do to get what I needed. Then things turned upside down with Rita, and I was robbing my own mama, stealing to buy the dope instead of selling it, smack instead of grass. Rita said, *Just once — you won't get hooked, and it's fine, so fine, better than the music, because it's inside.* She was right — it was better than the music, and it was inside: it made me forget the sound and the need.

Now my mama is singing me to sleep, humming near my ear, *Bless the child,* and I'm waking as a man twenty-one years old, and I'm going to Walpole till I'm thirty. Sweet-faced Rita has scrubbed herself clean for the trial. She says it was all my idea and she was afraid, who wouldn't be? Seven men see their own wives, their own daughters, and pray no man like me ever touches their pretty white things. They think they can put me away. They think locked doors and steel bars keep them safe. Five women see their own good selves and swear they'd never do what Rita did if not by force.

I want to tell them how different she can be, how she looks when she's strung out, too jittery to talk, when her jaw goes so tight the tendons pop in her neck. I want to tell them how she begged me, *Please Jimmy please,* how she said it was so easy, her old neighborhood, her own people, habits she could predict, dogs she could calm. I want to ask them, *Do black men drive your streets alone?* I want to tell them, *I was in the back, on the floor, covered by a blanket. She drove. She waited in the car, watching you, while I broke windows, emptied jewelry boxes, hunted furs.*

Next thing I know I'm in prison and she's on probation and

Mama's telling me, *You got to stay alive.* Ninety-two times she says it. Once a month for eight years, then one month she doesn't show, and the next week Bernice comes, says Mama's sick and aren't I ashamed. Then Mama comes again, three more times, but she's looking yellowish, not her high yellow but some new dirty yellow that even fills her eyes. She's not losing her weight but it's slipping down around her in strange ways, hanging heavy and low, so when she walks toward me, she looks like a woman dragging her own body. *My baby.* That's all she says. But I know the rest. Then Bernice is there again, shaking her head, telling me one more time how Mama gave up her life to give us a decent chance and she's got reason to be proud — little Leroy a schoolteacher, Bernice a nurse. I mean to remind her, *You feed mashed-up peas to old ladies with no teeth. You slip bedpans under wrinkled white asses. Wearing a uniform don't make you no nurse, Bernice.* But I just say, *Lucky for Mama the two of you turned out so fine.* I grin but Bernice isn't smiling; Bernice is crossing her big arms over her big chest. I see her fall to her knees as if her body is folding under her. I see her face crumple as if she's just been struck. And I'm not in prison. I'm free, but just barely, and I see my own dark hands in too-small white gloves, five other men like me, lifting the box and Mama in it, the light through stained glass glowing above us and that terrible wailing, the women crying but not Mama, the women singing as if they still believe in their all-merciful God, as if they've forgotten their sons: sacrificed, dead, in solitary, on the street, rotting in a jungle, needles in their arms, fans tied around their necks, as if they don't look up at Jesus and say, *What a waste.*

I remembered my own small hands in the other white gloves; I thought my skin would stain them. I would never be washed clean. But I was, baptized and redeemed. The white robes swirled, dragged me down, blinded me, and I thought, I can't swim, I'm going to die, and this is why my father wouldn't come to church today — the preacher in black is letting me die, is holding my head under, he wants me to die, it's necessary. I remember the stories my mother and I read, forbidden stories, our secret: cities crumbling, land scorched, plagues of frogs and gnats, plagues of boils and hail, seas and rivers turned to blood, and then, suddenly, I am rising and I am alive, spared by grace. The whole church trembles around me, women singing, telling Moses to let their people go, sweet low voices urging the children to wade in the water, but I know it's too deep, too dark, and I wasn't wading, I was drowning, but the voices are triumphant, the walls are tumbling down. Easter morning light blazes through colored glass; John baptizes Jesus above the water where we are baptized. I am shivering, cold, crying. Mama is sobbing too; I hear her voice above the others, but I know she's happy. I know that Jesus is alive again just as I am alive, and I have never been this clean, and I am going to be good forever, and I am going to love Jesus who has saved me through his suffering, and I am going to forgive my father who has forsaken me. I am high and righteous and without doubt. I am ten years old.

These same women are still singing about that same damn river, like this time they're really going to cross it, when everybody knows they're stuck here just like me and not one of us can swim; the only river we see is thick as oil and just as black, so what's the point of even trying when you'd be frozen stiff in two minutes and sinking like the bag of sticks and bones you are, and still they won't stop swaying, as if they have no bones, as if the air is water and they are under it, and they are swimming, and they cannot be drowned, as if women have a way of breathing that men don't. I'm choking. I look at Leroy to see if he's drowning too, to see if he's gasping, remembering Mama, our love for her, our guilt, but he's not guilty, he's a good clean boy, a teacher, clever little Leroy making numbers split in pieces, making them all come together right again. *Nothing can be lost*, he says, and he believes it. I say, *Didn't you ever want anything?* And he looks at me like I'm talking shit, which I suppose I am, but I still wonder, Why didn't you feel it, that buzz in your veins, the music playing; why didn't you ever close your eyes and forget who it was Mama told you not to touch? Didn't we have the same blind father? Didn't you ever wonder where Mama got her gold eyes? Didn't the rabbitman ever fly through your open window?

Twenty years now and I still want to ask my brother the same questions. Twenty years and I still want to tell our mama I'm sorry — but I know there are times *sorry* don't mean a thing. I want to ask her, *Do you blame me?* And I want to ask her, *Should I go out in the snow?* I almost hear her answer, but I don't go.

Digging graves, hauling garbage, snaking sewers — I've done every filthy job, and now, two years, something halfway decent, graveyard shift but no graves. It's good work, steady, because there are always broken windows, busted doors. Fires burst glass; cars jump curbs; bullets tear through locks; police crack wood — always — so I don't have to worry, and Mama would be proud.

I'm alone with it, boards and nails, the hammer pounding. I strike straight, hold the place in my mind, like Daddy said. It's winter. My bare hands split at the knuckles, my bare hands bleed in the cold. Wind burns my ears, but I don't mind. I

don't want anything — not money, not music, not a woman. I
know how desires come, one hooked to the other, and I'm glad
my heart is a fist, shattered on a prison wall, so I don't have to
think I might still play — because I can't, and it's not just the
bones broken. But sometimes I hear the sound underneath
the sound: it's summer, it's hot, the radios are blasting —
brothers rapping, Spanish boys pleading, bad girls bitching —
nobody knows a love song — then the gun goes off, far away,
and I hear that too, and later, sirens wailing. There's an argu-
ment downstairs, the Puerto Rican girl and her Anglo boyfriend, cursing in different languages. All those sounds are the
song, pieces of it, but I'm listening for the one sound below it
all, the one that pulls us down, the one that keeps us safe.
Then I catch it: it's the rain that's stopped — it's the cars
passing on the wet street — it's the soft hiss of tires through
water, and it almost breaks me.

If I could find Rita now I'd tell her she was right: junk is
better than jazz. It's fast and it doesn't hurt you the way the
music does. It's easy. It takes you and you don't have to do
anything. It holds you tighter than you've ever been held.
You think it loves you. It knows where to lick and when to
stop. When it hums in your veins, it says, *Don't worry, I'm with
you now.*

I'd tell her, The blues scare everybody. They make you remember things that didn't happen to you, make you feel your
bones aren't yours only — they've been splintered a thousand
times; the blood has poured out of you your whole life; the
rabbitman's skin is your skin and the body you share is on fire.
Or it's simpler than that, and you're just your own daddy, or
your own mama sitting beside him. Then you wish you didn't
have to feel what they feel, and you get your wish, and you're
nobody but your own self, watching.

Every beat I played was a step closer to my uncle's house, where I listened to my cousins breathe in the bed above me, where I slept on the floor because Daddy was blind in our house, Daddy's legs were swollen twice their size and stinking, Daddy was cut loose on his own poison and Mama was there, alone, with him — giving him whiskey, washing him, no matter what he said, no matter who he cursed.

My cousins take me to the woods — Lucy and Louise, one older, one younger. They say, *Touch me here, and here.* They dare me, they giggle. They touch *me* and make me forget what's happening across the field, in my house; then they run away and I hear the grasshoppers chirping all around me, buzzing — frantic, invisible — and then, I remember.

But smack, it makes you forget, it makes you not care, just like Rita said. It promises, *There's nothing more you need to know.* So I didn't have to see my father's never-clean clothes snapping on the line. I didn't have to remember Mama bent over the washtub in the yard, flesh of her arm quivering like she wanted to wash out evil as well as filth. I didn't have to go in the truck with Daddy that morning when he said it was time I saw my future. I didn't have to swing the sledgehammer with my boy's arms or see the bull's eyes, mad with disbelief.

But now I remember everything, how I struck the head but too close to the nose, so there was the crack and blood spouting from the mouth but no crumpling, and Daddy said, *Hold the place in your mind.* I swung a second time, grazed the face, and the bull swelled with his own breath, filling the stall. Three strikes in all before my father grabbed the hammer: one blow, and the animal folded, knees bending, neck sagging, the whole huge beast collapsing on itself.

Then the others came, sawed off head and legs, slit skin from flesh, peeled the animal — *strange fruit* — and there was blood, a river of it, hot, and there was blood, swirling at my feet. The body opened and there was blood weeping from the walls and the rabbitman ran so fast he ran out of his own skin and the bowels spilled, an endless rope, thick and heavy, full, and the smell, but the men work in the heat of the animal: kidneys, bladder, balls — saved, and the blood spatters them: faces, hands, thighs; they are soaked with it, I am soaked, I will never be clean, and even the ceiling is dripping until at last the carcass is hung on a hook in the cold room full of bodies without legs or heads or hearts.

But I am washed clean and I do forgive my father and my father dies and my grandparents forgive my mother for her bad marriage. I am fifteen. It's November, still warm in Virginia but not in Boston, which is where we're going, on the train, with my grandfather, who is kind enough but doesn't know us, who won't come inside our house, who's brought a suitcase full of clothes we have to wear and shoes that hurt our feet. He and Granny Booker mean to save us, mean to *compensate*. They say we can be anything. But all I want to be is the music, all I want to hear is the sound. Doctor Booker means I can be like him, and I think about that, the sharp razor's edge of his scalpel, all his delicate knives. I feel his clamps. I touch speculum and forceps, imagining how precisely he opens the body, what he finds there when he does. I see the familiar brown spatters on shirt cuffs and pants legs, his never-clean clothes, and I think, For all your pride, you're no better than my father, no different, and the distance from his house to yours is only the space in which a man turns around.

I remember my father crying. It frightened me more than anything, more than the bull, more than the water where I thought I'd drown. And this is all it was: scarecrow on a fence. He must have been going blind even then. He thought it was another one, body tangled in barbed wire. But it was only clothes stuffed with rags, pillowcase head tied off at the neck, straw hat and empty sleeves blowing in hot wind.

In prison I learned that my body itself is the enemy, my skin so black it reflects you. You want to take it from me. I terrify. Even when I am one and you are twenty. Even when I am cuffed and you have clubs. Even when I show you my empty hands and you show me your guns. I alarm you. I do what any animal will do: no matter how many times you strike, I try to stand. I mean to stay alive.

Which is why the girl in the street scared me. I thought, Maybe she's not a crackhead. Maybe she's just a woman from the other side, lost in another country, running deeper into it because once you're here you can't see your way out. Cross a road, walk under a bridge; that's how far. No signs, no stone wall, but the line's as tight as a border crossing. If you close your eyes it glitters like broken glass, pale and blue, a thousand shattered windshields. Here, every gesture is a code. Boys patrol their turf, four square blocks, pretend they own something. They travel in packs and arm themselves because they're more afraid than any of us, because every time they look up the sky is falling, so they're rapping about the cops they're gonna dust, the cities they're gonna torch. The little brothers are spinning on their heads, like this is some dance, some game — their bodies twist in ways they were never meant to bend, and then everybody in the street just falls down dead.

And the old men like me sit in the bars, drinking whiskey, going numb, talking about snatch and getting even all in the same breath, and we sound just like our own pitiful mamas, saying, *Judgment Day gonna come, righteous gonna be raised up, and the wicked gonna suffer, rich or poor, don't make no difference.* Except the men, the justice they're talking don't have nothing to do with God. They're full of the old words, saying, *We can't come in the house we're gonna knock it down;* then they sound just like the boys in the street, only tired and slurred, and the boys out there, they're quick, they got matches and gasoline, they talk fast as spit and don't ever need to sleep. But the flames burst at their backs, and they're the ones on fire.

We know the rules. Mess with white folks, you pay. Kill a white man, you hang. Kill a black man? That's just one more nigger off the street. So when I think about that girl, when I think, If she's still out there, she's in trouble, when I think even my mama would tell me I should go, I remind myself, I already done enough time for a white girl. I know how they are, how she'd be scared of me even if I said, *I just want to help you.* And I know how it would look in the alley — big black man's got his hands on a skinny white girl. Just my luck the boyfriend would come looking, shoot me dead. Nobody'd ask him why.

I think, Maybe she's already dead and I'll find her, touch her once and leave the perfect print of my hand burned on her thigh. I don't have a phone, and anyway, too late to call. They'd wanna know *Why'd you wait so long?*, and I'd be gone.

Last time they found a white woman dead on this hill police turned into a lynch mob, got the whole city screaming behind them. Roadblocks and strip searches. Stopped every dark-skinned man for miles if he was tall enough and not too old. Busted down doors, emptied closets, shredded mattresses, and never did find the gun that was already in the river. But they found the man they wanted: tall, raspy voice, like me. He's got a record, long, shot a police officer once. He's perfect. He can be sacrificed. No education, string of thefts. Even his own people are glad to turn him over, like there's some evil here and all we got to do is cut it out. I'm thinking, Nobody kills the woman and leaves the man alive. Even an ignorant nigger. But the police, they don't think that way. They need somebody. Turns out the husband did it. Shot his wife. Pregnant, too. Months later, white man jumps, bridge to river, January, he's dead, then everybody knows. But that black guy, he's still in jail. Violating parole. Some shit like that. Who knows? They got him, they're gonna keep him.

I hear two voices, and they both sound like my mama. One tells me, *She's human, go.* And one whispers, *You got to keep yourself alive.* One's my real mama and one a devil with my mama's voice.

Something howled. I thought it was the wind. I wanted to lean into it, wrap my arms around it. I wanted it to have a mouth, to swallow me. Or I wanted to swallow it, to cry as it cried, loud and blameless.

It was nearly dawn and I was ashamed, knowing now which voice belonged to my mama. I held the girl in my mind. She was light as a moth, bright as a flame. I knew she was dead. It was as if she'd called my name, my real one, the one I didn't know until she spoke it. I felt her lungs filling under my hand. She said, *There's one warm place at the center of my body where I wait for you.*

Stray finds her. Mangy wolf of a dog. Smells her. Even in this cold, he knows. And it's like he loves her, the way he calls, just whining at first, these short yelps, high and sad, and when nobody comes he starts howling, loud enough to wake the dead, I think, but not her. And it's day, the first one.

We're out there in the cold, nine of us in the alley, hunched, hands in pockets, no hats, shivering, shaking our heads, and one guy is saying, Shit, *shit*, because he remembers, we all remember, the last time.

I see her close, thirty-five at least but small, so I thought she was a girl, and I think of her that way now. I kneel beside her. Her eyes are open, irises shattered like blue glass. Wind ruffles her nightgown, exposes her. Snow blows through her hair, across bare legs, between blue lips. I see bruises on her thighs, cuts on her hands, a face misaligned, and I think, I have bones like these, broken, healed, never the same. My hand aches in the cold.

I know now what happened, why she's here. I see her keeper. She smokes his cigarettes, he whacks her. She drinks his beer, he drags her to the toilet, holds her head in the bowl. He's sorry. I've heard the stories. I've seen the women. And I've been slammed against a cement wall for looking the man in the eye. I've been kicked awake at three A.M. because some motherfucker I offended told the guards I had a knife. The keepers make the rules, but they're always shifting: we can't be good enough.

Police stay quiet. Don't want to look like fools again. And nobody's asking for this girl. Stray, like the dog. They got time.

I know now what her body tells them: stomach empty, liver enlarged, three ribs broken, lacerations on both hands — superficial wounds, old bruises blooming like yellow flowers on her back and thighs. Death by exposure. No crime committed here. And they don't care who cut her, and they don't care who broke her ribs, because all her people are dead or don't give a shit, and she was the one, after all, who ran out in the snow, so who's to say she didn't want to die.

I drink port because it's sweet, gin because it's bitter, back to back, one kills the taste of the other. I can't get drunk. Three days now since we found her and I see her whole life, like she's my sister and I grew up with her. She's a child with a stick drawing pictures in the dirt. She's drawn a face and I think it must be her own face but I say, *What are you drawing?* And she says, *Someone to love me.* I say, *What are you trying to do, break my heart?* And she says, *If you have a heart, I'll break it.* I say, *Where's your mama?* And she says, *She's that pretty lady with red lips and high heels — you've probably seen her — but sometimes her lipstick's smeared all down her chin and her stockings are ripped and she's got one shoe in her hand and the spike is flying toward me — that's my mother.* I say, *Where's your daddy?* And she says, *He's a flannel shirt torn at the shoulder hanging in the closet ever since I've been alive and my mother says that's the reason why.*

Then I see she's not a child; she's a full-grown woman, and her hands are cut, her hands are bleeding, and I say, *Who did this to you?* She won't answer, but I know, I see him, he's her lover, he's metal flashing, he's a silver blade in the dark, and she tries to grab him but he's too sharp. Then she's running, she's crying, and I see her in the street, and I think she's just some crazy white girl too high to feel the cold, and I don't go.

Now she's talking to me always. She's the sound underneath all other sounds. She won't go away. She says, *I used to make angels in the snow, like this; I used to lie down, move my arms and legs, like this, wings and skirt, but that night I was too cold, so I just lay down, curled into myself, see, here, and I saw you at your window, and I knew you were afraid, and I wanted to tell you, I'm always afraid, but after I lay down I wasn't so cold, and I was almost happy, and I was almost asleep, but I wanted to tell you, I'm your little white sister — I know you — we're alone.*

N O B O D Y ' S

D A U G H T E R S

I waited for you in the rain. My tongue hurt. I'd been telling lies all day. Lies to the four Christian teenagers who thought they could save me. My first ride, Albany to Oneonta — they sang the whole way. More lies to the jittery pink-skinned man who took me north. He offered tiny blue pills and fat black ones. He said, *It's safe — don't worry — I'm a nurse.* He said, *I'll make you feel good.*

I think I had a sister once. Everywhere I go she's been before me. There's no getting out of it.

When the pink nurse stopped to piss, my sister Clare whispered, *Look at him — he'll kill you if he can.* I hid in the woods by the lake full of stumps. I didn't move. I let the sky pour through me. He called the name I'd said was mine. Sometimes I heard branches breaking. Sometimes only rain. Finally he yelled at me, at who he thought I was. He said, *No more games.* He said, *Fine, freeze your ass.* His voice cracked. I could have chosen him instead of you, but Clare breathed on my hands. She said, *He doesn't have anything you want.*

You were driving toward me, your blue truck still hours away. Cold rain, cars whipping water — only my faith made me wait. I swear I knew you, your soft beard, how it would be. But you never imagined us together. You never meant to stop for me.

This I won't tell. This you'll never know. Mick says I'm fourteen going on forty. I've got that dusty skin, dry, my eyes kind of yellowish where they're supposed to be white. It's the rum I drink, and maybe my kidneys never did work that well. Mick, who is my mother's husband now, says I'll be living on the street at sixteen, dead at twenty. He says this to me, when we're alone. Once I paid two dollars, let Mama Rosa read my palm to see if he was right, and she told me I was going to outlive everyone I love.

I know I'm strange. I drift. Maybe I'm smoking a cigarette, leaning on the bricks. Somebody's talking. Then I'm not there. I'm a window breaking. I'm pieces of myself falling on the ground. Later I wake up in my own body and my fingers are burned.

Clare says, *Just stand up.*

She's careless, my sister. She gets drunk. She puts other people's blood in her veins. Her skin's hot. She goes out in the cold without her coat and waits for her lover to come. Wind drives snow in her face. Ice needles her bare arms. Some night she'll lie down in the woods and he won't find her. Some night she'll lie down in the road.

It's November. I know because there are Halloween men rotting in all the yards, snagged on fences, skewered on poles. Pumpkin heads scooped hollow — they stink of their own spoiled selves. One boy's stuck in a tree. His head's a purple cabbage. You could peel him down to his brainless core.

I know some men downtown, Halloween men trying to walk on stuffed legs. Rags on sticks, pants full of straw, foul wind blowing through them to scare the crows. I think they made themselves. They have those eyes. Carved. Candles guttering inside their soft skulls.

They live in a brick house you can't blow down — boards instead of windows, nails in the doors. They tell me, *Come alone.*

They have dusted joints and I have seven dollars. They have pocketsful of pills and I have pennies I found in the snow. I know how easy it is to go down the steps to the basement, to stand shivering against the wall. Nothing hurts me. Earl says, *Pain is just a feeling like any other feeling.* He should know. *Knife, slap, kiss, flame.* He says, *Forget their names and they pass through you.* Earl has wooden arms and metal hands. His left ear's a hole, his nose a bulb of flesh from somewhere else. He sits in the corner and smokes. He holds the joint in his silver claw. His long feet are always bare. When he whispers in his half-voice, everything stops.

No money the night before I found you. One of the Halloween men said, *Come with me.* He had pink hearts and poppers. He knew I'd need them. He said, *It's dangerous to sleep.* I looked at Earl. I thought his lips moved. I thought he said, *Nothing lasts too long.*

This speedboy with poppers was the whitest man I ever saw. When I closed my eyes he was a white dog bounding through streets of snow. I tried not to think of his skin, all of it, how bright it was, how his body exposed would blind me, how his white palms blazed against my hips. I thought of Earl instead, smooth arms, cool hands, Earl who only burned himself, hair flaming around soft ears, holy angel, face melting into bone.

Clare said, *Nobody will find you.*

The whiteman was in me, close enough to hear; he said, *Not even God.*

God doesn't like to watch little girls pressed against basement walls. God doesn't like little girls who swallow pills and drink rum. God's too old to get down on his hands and knees and peer through the slats of boards. Glass broken long ago but shards still on the ground. He might cut his palms. If he ever thinks of me, maybe he'll send his son.

I never slept with the whiteman.

I mean, I never lay down and closed my eyes.

Clare said, *There's no reason to go home.* She made me remember the trailer in December, a ring of Christmas lights blinking its outline, red and green and gold, the wet snow the first winter she was gone. She made me remember the white ruffled curtains on the windows and the three plastic swans in the yard. She said she hitched two hundred miles once to stand outside, to watch us inside, the fog of our breath on the glass. She said our mother had a new husband and two sons. She said we were nobody's daughters. She said, *They all want you to go.*

Singing Christians, pink nurse, rain — I waited, saw your blue truck at last. I had a dream once of your body, damp hair of your chest, my fingers in it. As soon as you stopped, I remembered the hunting cap on the seat between us, the rabbit fur inside your gloves.

I surprised you. I'm the living proof: unknown father's daughter. Tall bony Nadine. Dark-eyed Nadine. Girl from the lake of stumps. Water swirling in a mother's dream. His face rising toward her. Shadow of a hand making the sign of the cross.

I pulled the blanket from my head and you saw the holes in my ear — you counted the tarnished hoops, nine, cartilage to lobe.

Later I'll show you: the holes in my ear never hurt like the hole in my tongue.

You were amazed by the space I filled — long legs, muddy boots; you had no reason to let the wet-wool, black-hair smell of me into your warm truck. Moments before, I looked small and helpless, a child on the road, no bigger than your own daughter, ten years old, her impossibly thin arms, all her fragile breakable bones.

I closed my eyes so you wouldn't be afraid. I was just a girl again, alone, but the smell — it filled the cab; you breathed me; I was in your lungs. I was your boyself, the bad child, the one who ran away from you, the one you never found.

Later there was fog and dark, the rain, heavy. You didn't know where we were going. You didn't know where to stop. The lights of cars coming toward us exploded in mist, blinding you. I said, *Pull over.* I said, *We can wait it out.*

And it was there, in the fog, in the rain, in the terrifying light of cars still coming, that I kissed you the first time. It was there parked on the soft gravel shoulder that I stuck my pierced tongue in your mouth and you put your hands under my shirt to feel my ribs, the first time. It was there that you said, *Careful, baby,* and you meant my tongue, the stud — it hurt you — and I thought of the handcuffs in my bag, stolen from the Halloween man, the last one, the white one — he was cursing me even now. I could have cuffed you to your wheel, left you to explain. I imagined myself in your coat, carrying your gun.

But I loved you.

I mean, I didn't want to go.

The rain slowed. The fog blew across the road. You drove. I wore your gloves, felt the fur of the animal around every finger. I stared at the lights till my eyes were holes.

You were tired. You were sorry. It was too late to throw me

out. You said we'd stop at a motel. You said we'd sleep. You said, *What happened back there — don't worry.* You meant it wasn't going to go any further. You meant you thought it was your fault.

I disgusted you now. I saw that. Your tongue hurt. My sour breath was in your mouth. *Never,* you thought, *not with her.* Dirty Nadine. Nothing like my pretty sister. Pale half-sister. Daughter of the father before my father. Not like Clare, lovely despite her filth, delicate Clare, thin as your daughter — you could hold her down. You could take her to any room. You could wash her. You could break her with one blow. You would never guess how dangerous she is. You can't see the shadows on her lungs, her hard veins, her brittle bones. You can't see the bloom of blood. Later I'll tell you about the handprints on all the doors of the disappeared. Later I'll explain the lines of her open palm.

Is she alive? Try to find her. Ask her yourself.

Never is the car door slamming. *Never* is the key in the lock, the Traveler's Rest Motel, the smell of disinfectant, the light we don't turn on. *Never* is the mattress so old you feel the coils against your back when you fall. My tongue's in your mouth. Your cock's hard against my thigh. *Never.*

Clare has a game. We strobe. She grabs my hand, sticks the wire in the socket. She dares me to hang on.

I'm a thief. It's true.

I turn you into a thief. It's necessary. You'll think of that forever, the sheet you had to steal to get out of the motel. You'll remember your bare legs in the truck, the cold vinyl through thin cloth, the white half-moon hanging in the morning sky, face down.

Days now and hundreds of miles since I left you. You wear

your orange vest, carry your oiled gun. You follow tracks in snow. I follow Clare to the road. She wants me to find her, to feel what she feels, to do everything she's done.

When you see the doe at last, you think of me. You're alone with me — there's no one you can tell about the girl on the road, her sore tongue in your mouth. *Never,* you said, *no* and *no,* but you twitched under her, blinded by the flickering in your skull. No one will understand. You thought her hands would turn you inside out, but you held on. There's no one you can tell about the wallet she opened, the cash and pictures, the pants she stole.

Careful, baby.

I've got your life now — your little girl smiling in my hand, dressed in her white fairy costume, waving her sparkling fairy wand; I hold your sad wife in her striped bathing suit. If I could feel, her chubby knees would break my heart. I've got you in my pocket — your driver's license, my proof. I'm in your pants. I belt them tight. I keep your coins in my boots for good luck. I wear your hat, earflaps down. I bought a silver knife with your forty-three dollars. I carved your name in a cross on my thigh.

Yesterday I found a dump of jack-o'-lanterns in the ditch, the smashed faces of all the men I used to know. They grinned to show me the stones in their broken mouths. They've taken themselves apart. I'm looking for their unstuffed clothes, hoping they didn't empty their pockets before their skulls flamed out.

It's dark. Clare pulls me toward the gully. She wants me to run down between the black trees and twisting vines. She wants me to feel my way — she wants me to crawl.

Morning again, I saw a deer, only the head and legs, bits of hide, a smear of blood, five crows taking flight, wings hissing as they rose. Someone's accident butchered here, the stunned meat taken home. Before you fell asleep, I said, *Anyone can kill.*

She's in your sights. Nobody understands your fear, how you feel my hands even now, reaching for your wrists, slipping under your clothes. So many ways to do it, brutal or graceful, silent as the blood in my sister's veins or full of shattered light and sound. Kick to the shoulder, blast of the gun — she staggers, wounded, not killed all at once. There's snow on the ground, gold leaves going brown. There's light in the last trembling leaves but the sun is gone. You follow her trail, dark puddles spreading in snow, black into white, her blood.

You remember a farmer straddling his own sheep. *Will it be like this?* The knife, one slit, precise. *Pain is just a feeling like any other feeling.* She never struggled. He reached inside, grabbed something, squeezed hard. *I can't tell you what it was.*

She won't drop in time, won't give up. When you put your hands in front of you, you almost feel her there: hair, flesh, breath, blood. She wants only what you want: to survive one minute more.

What would you do if you found her now, if her ragged breathing stopped? Too far to drag her back to the truck; you'd have to open her in the sudden dark, pull her steaming entrails into the snow.

I wait for the next ride. Clare wants me to follow in her tracks, to find her before she falls, to touch her, to wash her blood clean in this snow, to put it back in her veins, to make her whole.

You walk in a circle. You wonder if you're lost. The doe's following you now, but at a distance. She's trying to forgive you. If she could speak, she might tell you the way home. She might say, *You can climb inside me, wear my body like a coat.*

You can't explain this to anyone. *Never, no.* You need me. I'm the only one alive who knows your fear, who understands how dangerous we are to each other in these woods, on this road.

2 ⟨ X M A S ,   J A M A I C A   P L A I N

I'm your worst fear.

But not the worst thing that can happen.

I lived in your house half the night. I'm the broken window in your little boy's bedroom. I'm the flooded tiles in the bathroom where the water flowed and flowed.

I'm the tattoo in the hollow of Emile's pelvis, five butterflies spreading blue wings to rise out of his scar.

I'm dark hands slipping through all your pale woman underthings; dirty fingers fondling a strand of pearls, your throat, a white bird carved of stone. I'm the body you feel wearing your fox coat.

Clare said, *Take the jewelry; it's yours.*

My heart's in my hands: what I touch, I love; what I love, I own.

Snow that night and nobody seemed surprised, so I figured it must be winter. Later I remembered it was Christmas, or it had been, the day before. I was with Emile, who wanted to be Emilia. We'd started downtown, Boston. Now it was Jamaica Plain, three miles south. *Home for the holidays,* Emile said, some private joke. He'd been working the block around the Greyhound Station all night, wearing nothing but a white scarf and black turtleneck, tight jeans. *Man wants to see before he buys,* Emile said. He meant the ones in long cars, cruising, looking for fragile boys with female faces.

Emile was sixteen, he thought.

Getting old.

He'd made sixty-four dollars, three tricks with cash, plus some pills — a bonus for good work, blues and greens, he didn't know what. Nobody'd offered to take him home, which is all he wanted: a warm bed, some sleep, eggs in the morning, the smell of butter, hunks of bread torn off the loaf.

Crashing, both of us, ragged from days of speed and crack, no substitute for the smooth high of pure cocaine but all we could afford. Now, enough cash between us at last. I had another twenty-five from the man who said he was in the circus once, who called himself the Jungle Creep — on top of me he made that sound. Before he unlocked the door, he said, *Are you a real girl?* I looked at his plates — New Jersey; that's why he didn't know the lines, didn't know that the boys as girls stay away from the Zone unless they want their faces crushed. He wanted me to prove it first. Some bad luck once, I guess. I said, *It's fucking freezing. I'm real. Open the frigging door or go.*

Now it was too late to score, too cold, nobody on the street but Emile and me, the wind, so we walked, we kept walking. I had a green parka, somebody else's wallet in the pocket — I couldn't remember who or where, the coat stolen weeks ago and still mine, a miracle out here. We shared, trading it off. I loved Emile. I mean, it hurt my skin to see his cold.

Emile had a plan. It had to be Jamaica Plain, *home* — enough hands as dark as mine, enough faces as brown as Emile's — not like Brookline, where we'd have to turn ourselves inside out. Jamaica Plain, where there were pretty painted houses next to shacks, where the sound of bursting glass wouldn't be that loud.

Listen, we needed to sleep, to eat, that's all. So thirsty even my veins felt dry, flattened out. Hungry somewhere in my head, but my stomach shrunken to a knot so small I thought it might be gone. I remembered the man, maybe last week, before the snow, leaning against the statue of starved horses, twisted metal at the edge of the Common. He had a knife, long enough for gutting fish. Dressed in camouflage but not hiding. He stared at his thumb, licked it clean, and cut deep to watch the bright blood bubble out. He stuck it in his mouth to drink, hungry, and I swore I'd never get that low. But nights later I dreamed him beside me. Raw and dizzy, I woke, offering my whole hand, begging him to cut it off.

We walked around your block three times. We were patient now. Numb. No car up your drive and your porch light blazing, left to burn all night, we thought. Your house glowed, yellow even in the dark, paint so shiny it looked wet, and Emile said he lived somewhere like this once, when he was still a boy all the time, hair cropped short, before lipstick and mascara, when his cheeks weren't blushed, before his mother caught him and his father locked him out.

In this house Emile found your red dress, your slippery stockings. He was happy, I swear.

So why did he end up on the floor?

I'm not going to tell you; I don't know.

First, the rock wrapped in Emile's scarf, glass splintering in the cold, and we climbed into the safe body of your house. Later we saw this was a child's room, your only one. We found the tiny cowboy boots in the closet, black like Emile's but small, so small. I tried the little bed. It was soft enough but too short. In every room your blue-eyed boy floated on the wall. Emile wanted to take him down. Emile said, *He scares me.* Emile said your little boy's too pretty, his blond curls too long. Emile said, *Some night the wrong person's going to take him home.*

Emile's not saying anything now, but if you touched his mouth you'd know. Like a blind person reading lips, you'd feel everything he needed to tell.

We stood in the cold light of the open refrigerator, drinking milk from the carton, eating pecan pie with our hands, squirting whipped cream into our mouths. You don't know how it hurt us to eat this way, our shriveled stomachs stretching; you don't know why we couldn't stop. We took the praline ice cream to your bed, one of those tiny containers, sweet and sickening, bits of candy frozen hard. We fell asleep and it melted, so we drank it, thick, with your brandy, watching bodies writhe on the TV, no sound: flames and ambulances all night; children leaping; a girl in mud under a car, eight men lifting; a skier crashing into a wall — we never knew who was saved and who was not. Talking heads spit the news again and again. There was no reason to listen — tomorrow exactly the same things would happen, and still everyone would forget.

There were other houses after yours, places where I went alone, but there were none before and none like this. When I want to feel love I remember the dark thrill of it, the bright sound of glass, the sudden size and weight of my own heart in my own chest, how I knew it now, how it was real to me in my body, separate from lungs and liver and ribs, how it made the color of my blood surge against the back of my eyes, how nothing mattered anymore because I believed in this, my own heart, its will to live.

No lights, no alarm. We waited outside. Fifteen seconds.

Years collapsed. We were scared of you, who you might be inside, terrified lady with a gun, some fool with bad aim and dumb luck. The boost to the window, Emile lifting me, then I was there, in you, I swear, the smell that particular, that strong, almost a taste in your boy's room, his sweet milky breath under my tongue. Heat left low, but to us warm as a body, humid, hot.

My skin's cracked now, hands that cold, but I think of them plunged deep in your drawer, down in all your soft under- belly underclothes, slipping through all your jumbled silky womanthings.

I pulled them out and out.

I'm your worst fear. I touched everything in your house: all the presents just unwrapped — cashmere sweater, rocking horse, velvet pouch. I lay on your bed, smoking cigarettes, wrapped in your fur coat. How many foxes? I tried to count.

But it was Emile who wore the red dress, who left it crum- pled on the floor.

Thin as he is, he couldn't zip the back — he's a boy, after all — he has those shoulders, those soon-to-be-a-man bones. He swore trying to squash his boy feet into the matching heels; then he sobbed. I had to tell him he had lovely feet, and he did, elegant, long — those golden toes. I found him a pair of stockings, one size fits all.

I wore your husband's pinstriped jacket. I pretended all the gifts were mine to offer. I pulled the pearls from their violet pouch.

We danced.

We slid across the polished wooden floor of your living room, spun in the white lights of the twinkling tree. And again, I tell you, I swear I felt the exact size and shape of things inside me, heart and kidney, my sweet left lung. All the angels hanging from the branches opened their glass mouths, stunned.

He was more woman than you, his thick hair wound tight and pinned. *Watch this,* he said, *chignon.*

I'm not lying. He transformed himself in front of your mirror, gold eyeshadow, faint blush. He was beautiful. He could have fooled anyone. Your husband would have paid a hundred dollars to feel Emile's mouth kiss all the places you won't touch.

Later the red dress lay like a wet rag on the floor. Later the stockings snagged, the strand of pearls snapped and the beads rolled. Later Emile was all boy, naked on the bathroom floor.

I'm the one who got away, the one you don't know; I'm the long hairs you find under your pillow, nested in your drain, tangled in your brush. You think I might come back. You dream me dark always. I could be any dirty girl on the street, or the one on the bus, black lips, just-shaved head. You see her through mud-spattered glass, quick, blurred. You want me dead — it's come to this — killed, but not by your clean hands. You pray for accidents instead, me high and spacy, stepping off the curb, a car that comes too fast. You dream some twisted night road and me walking, some poor drunk weaving his way home. He won't even know what he's struck. In the morning he'll touch the headlight I smashed, the fender I splattered, dirt or blood. In the light he'll see my body rising, half remembered, snow that whirls to a shape then blows apart. Only you will know for sure, the morning news, another unidentified girl dead, hit and run, her killer never found.

I wonder if you'll rest then, or if every sound will be glass, every pair of hands mine, reaching for your sleeping son.

How can I explain?

We didn't come for him.

I'm your worst fear. Slivers of window embedded in carpet. Sharp and invisible. You can follow my muddy footprints through your house, but if you follow them backward they always lead here: to this room, to his bed.

If you could see my hands, not the ones you imagine but my real hands, they'd be reaching for Emile's body. If you looked at Emile's feet, if you touched them, you could feel us dancing.

This is all I want.

After we danced, we lay so close on your bed I dreamed we were twins, joined forever this way, two arms, three legs, two heads.

But I woke in my body alone.

Outside, snow fell like pieces of broken light.

I already knew what had happened. But I didn't want to know.

I heard him in the bathroom.

I mean, I heard the water flow and flow.

I told myself he was washing you away, your perfume, your lavender oil scent. Becoming himself. Tomorrow we'd go.

I tried to watch the TV, the silent man in front of the map, the endless night news. But there it was, my heart again, throbbing in my fingertips.

I couldn't stand it — the snow outside; the sound of water; your little boy's head propped on the dresser, drifting on the wall; the man in the corner of the room, trapped in the flickering box: his silent mouth wouldn't stop.

I pounded on the bathroom door. I said, *Goddamn it, Emile, you're clean enough.* I said I had a bad feeling about this place. I said I felt you coming home.

But Emile, he didn't say a word. There was only water, that

one sound, and I saw it seeping under the door, leaking into the white carpet. Still I told lies to myself. I said, *Shit, Emile — what's going on?* I pushed the door. I had to shove hard, squeeze inside, because Emile was there, you know, exactly where you found him, face down on the floor. I turned him over, saw the lips smeared red, felt the water flow.

I breathed into him, beat his chest. It was too late, God, I know, his face pressed to the floor all this time, his face in the water, Emile dead even before he drowned, your bottle of Valium empty in the sink, the foil of your cold capsules punched through, two dozen gone — this is what did it: your brandy, your Valium, your safe little pills bought in a store. After all the shit we've done — smack popped under the skin, speed laced with strychnine, monkey dust — it comes to this. After all the nights on the streets, all the knives, all the pissed-off johns, all the fag-hating bullies prowling the Fenway with their bats, luring boys like Emile into the bushes with prom-ises of sex. After all that, this is where it ends: on your clean wet floor.

Above the thunder of the water, Clare said, *He doesn't want to live.*

Clare stayed very calm. She said, *Turn off the water, go.*

I kept breathing into him. I watched the butterflies between his bones. No flutter of wings and Clare said, *Look at him. He's dead.* Clare said she should know.

She told me what to take and where it was: sapphire ring, ivory elephant, snakeskin belt. She told me what to leave, what was too heavy: the carved bird, white stone. She re-minded me, *Take off that ridiculous coat.*

I knew Clare was right; I thought, Yes, everyone is dead: the silent heads in the TV, the boy on the floor, my father who can't be known. I thought even you might be dead — your husband asleep at the wheel, your little boy asleep in the back, only you awake to see the car split the guardrail and soar.

I saw a snow-filled ravine, your car rolling toward the river of thin ice.

I thought, You never had a chance.

But I felt you.

I believed in you. Your family. I heard you going from room to room, saying, *Who's been sleeping in my bed?*

It took all my will.

I wanted to love you. I wanted you to come home. I wanted you to find me kneeling on your floor. I wanted the wings on Emile's hips to lift him through the skylight. I wanted him to scatter: ash, snow. I wanted the floor dry, the window whole.

I swear, you gave me hope.

Clare knew I was going to do something stupid. Try to clean this up. Call the police to come for Emile. Not get out. She had to tell me everything. She said again, *Turn the water off.*

In the living room the tree still twinkled, the angels still hung. I remember how amazed I was they hadn't thrown themselves to the floor.

I remember running, the immaculate cold, the air in me, my lungs hard.

I remember thinking, I'm alive, a miracle anyone was. I wondered who had chosen me.

I remember trying to list all the decent things I'd ever done.

I remember walking till it was light, knowing if I slept, I'd freeze. I never wanted so much not to die.

I made promises, I suppose.

In the morning I walked across a bridge, saw the river frozen along the edges, scrambled down. I glided out on it; I walked on water. The snowflakes kept getting bigger and big-ger, butterflies that fell apart when they hit the ground, but the sky was mostly clear and there was sun.

Later, the cold again, wind and clouds. Snow shrank to ice. Small, hard. I saw a car idling, a child in the back, the driver standing on a porch, knocking at a door. Clare said, *It's open.* She meant the car. She said, *Think how fast you can go.* She told me I could ditch the baby down the road.

I didn't do it.

Later I stole lots of things, slashed sofas, pissed on floors.

But that day, I passed one thing by; I let one thing go.

When I think about this, the child safe and warm, the mother not wailing, not beating her head on the wall to make herself stop, when I think about the snow that day, wings in the bright sky, I forgive myself for everything else.

3 (HOME

November again. Harvard Square. I called Adele. Not the first time. One ring, two — never more than this. If my mother loved me, she'd pick it up that quick.

Don't be stupid, Clare said.

No answer, no surprise. Coins clanging down. *Jackpot,* Clare said.

I saw Emile across the street. He was a Latino boy with cropped hair, reaching for his mother's hand.

Then it was December third. I remember because afterward I looked at a paper in a box so I'd know exactly when.

One ring. My mother there, whispering in my ear.

Now you've done it, Clare said.

Past noon, Adele still fogged. I knew everything from the

sound of her voice, too low, knew she must be on night shift again: nursing home or bar, bringing bedpans or beers — it didn't matter which. I saw the stumps of cigarettes in the ashtray beside her bed. I saw her red hair matted flat, creases in her cheek, the way she'd slept. I smelled her, the smoke in her clothes, the smoke on her breath. I remembered her kissing me one night before I knew any words — that smell: lipstick and gin. I heard Clare sobbing in the bunk above mine, her face shoved into her pillow, and then our mother was gone — we were alone in the dark, and if I'd had any words I would have said, *Not again.*

Who is it? Sharper now, my mother, right in my hand. A weird warm day, so the Haitian man was playing his guitar by the Out Of Town News stand. He'd been dancing for hours, brittle legs, bobbing head. You never saw a grown man that thin. Sometimes he sang in French, and that's when I understood him best, when his voice passed through me, hands through water, when the words stopped making sense.

I wanted to hold out the phone, let my mother hear what I heard. I wanted to say, *Find me if you can.*

It's me, Nadine, I said.

I heard the match scrape, the hiss of flame burning air. I heard my mother suck in her breath.

Your daughter, I almost said.

Where are you?

I thought she was afraid I might be down the road, already on my way, needing money, her soft bed. I saw her there on the edge of the bunk, yellow spread wrapped around her shoulders, cigarette dangling from her lips. I saw the faded outlines of spilled coffee, dark stains on pale cloth, my mother's jittery hand.

Not that close, I said.

Muffled words. I thought she said, *I'm glad.* The Haitian man kept jumping, dreadlocks twisting, pants flapping — those legs, no flesh, another scarecrow man. Dollar bills fluttered in his guitar case, wings in wind. *Un coeur d'oiseaux brisés,* he said, and I almost knew what he meant. A crowd had gathered to listen, two dozen, maybe more, all those people between us, but he was watching me; I was watching him.

I'm glad you called, my mother said again.

And I swear, I knew then.

Je ne pleure pas, the Haitian man said.

For a moment both his feet were off the ground at once. For a moment his mouth stayed open, stunned. He was a dark angel hanging in blue air. I saw his heart break against his ribs. For a moment there were no cars and no breath.

Then every sound that ever was rushed in. Horns blaring, exploding glass; ice cracking on the river; *On the ground, motherfucker* — all this again.

I said, *Clare's dead.*

Tell me where you are, Nadine.

Fuck you, Clare said.

The Haitian man fell to earth. I heard the bones of his legs snap. He wouldn't look at me now. He was bent over his case, stuffing bills in his pockets.

The voice came over the phone, the one that says you have thirty seconds left. I said, *I'm out of quarters.* I said, *Maybe I'll call you back.*

That night I found a lover.

I mean, I found a man who didn't pay, who let me sleep in his car instead. He told me his name and I forget. Fat man with a snake coiled in the hair of his chest. I kept thinking, All this flesh. When he was in me, I thought I could be him.

Clare said, *I tried to come home once, but the birds had eaten all the crumbs. There was no path.*

The next night, another lover, another man with gifts. Two vials of crack we smoked, then heroin to cut the high. *Got to chase the dragon,* he said. No needles. Clean white smack so pure we only had to breathe it in. *Safe this way,* he said. He held a wet cloth, told me, *Lean back,* made me snort the water too, *got to get the last bit.* When he moved on top of me, I didn't have a body: I was all head.

Then it was day and I was drifting, knowing that by dark I'd have to look again.

Emile appeared on Newbury Street, shop window, second floor: he was a beautiful mannequin in a red dress.

Listen, you think it's easy the way we live? Clare told me this: *I never had a day off. I had to keep walking. I could never stay in bed.*

So she was glad when they put her in a cell, glad to give them all she had: clothes, cash, fingerprints. She said, *I knew enough not to drink the water, but nobody told me not to breathe the air.*

No lover that night. I found a cardboard box instead. Cold before dawn, and I thought, *Just one corner, just the edge.* When the flames burst, I meant to smother them. I felt Earl, his cool metal grasp. *Get out,* he said. Ashes floated in the frozen air, the box gone that fast. Clare said, *Look at me: this is what they did.* Later my singed hair broke off in my hands.

In the morning, I called Adele again. *Tell me,* I said.

I thought she might know exactly where and when. I thought there might be a room, a white sheet, a bed, a place I could enter and leave, the before and after of my sister's death.

But there were only approximate details, a jail, stones, barbed wire somewhere.

No body. She meant she never saw Clare dead.

Clare said she tried to get home in time, but the witch caught her and put her in the candy house instead.

Busted. Prostitution and possession.

Let me answer the charges.

This is Clare's story.

Let me tell you what my sister owned.

In her pocket, one vial of crack, almost gone. In her veins, strangers' blood. She possessed ninety-six pounds. I want to be exact. The ninety-six pounds included the weight of skin, coat, bowels, lungs; the weight of dirt under her nails; the weight of semen, three men last night and five the night before.

The ninety-six pounds included the vial, a rabbit's foot rubbed so often it was nearly hairless, worn to bone.

Around her wrist she wore her own hair, what was left of it, what she'd saved and braided, a bracelet now. In her left ear, one gold hoop and one rhinestone stud, and they didn't weigh much but were included in the ninety-six pounds.

She possessed the virus.

But did not think of it as hers alone.

She passed it on and on.

Stripped and showered, she possessed ninety-one pounds, her body only, which brings me to the second charge.

Listen, I heard of a man who gave a kidney to his brother. They hadn't spoken for eleven years. A perfect match in spite of this. All that blood flowed between them, but the brother died, still ranting, still full of piss and spit.

Don't talk to me about mercy.

The one who lived, the one left unforgiven, the one carved nearly in half, believed in justice of another kind: *If we possess our bodies only, we must offer up this gift.*

You can talk forever about risk.

New York City, Clare. Holding pen. They crammed her in a room, two hundred bodies close, no windows here. They told her to stand and stand, no ventilation, only a fan beating the poison air. And this is where she came to possess the mutant germ, the final gift. It required no consensual act, no exchange of blood or semen, no mother's milk, no generous brother willing to open his flesh.

Listen, who's coughing there?

All you have to do is breathe it in.

It loved her, this germ. It loved her lungs, first and best, the damp dark, the soft spaces there. But in the end, it wanted all of her and had no fear.

December still, Clare eight months dead. Adele knew only half of this.

You can always come home, she said.

I went looking for my lover, the fat one with the car, anybody with a snake on his chest.

I found three men in the Zone, all with cash — no snakes and none that fat. Tomorrow I'd look again. I wanted one with white skin and black hair, a belly where my bones could sink so I wouldn't feel so thin. I wanted the snake in my hands, the snake around my neck; I wanted his unbelievable weight to keep me pinned.

Ten days in a cell, Clare released. Two hundred and fifty-three hours without a fix — she thought she might go straight, but it didn't happen like that.

She found a friend instead. *You're sad, baby,* he said. She dropped her pants. Not for sex, not with him, only to find a vein not scarred too hard. When your blood blooms in the syringe, you know you've hit.

Listen, nobody asks to be like this.

If the dope's too pure, you're dead.

This is Clare's story. This is her voice speaking through me. This is my body. This is how we stay alive out here.

Listen. *It's hope that kills you in the end.*

On Brattle Street I saw this: tall man with thick legs, tiny child clutching his pants. Too beautiful, I thought, blue veins, fragile skull, her pulse flickering at the temple where I could touch it if I dared. The man needed a quarter for the meter. He asked me for change, held out three dimes. *A good trade,* I said. He stepped back toward the car, left the girl between us. I crouched to be her size, spoke soft words, nonsense, and she stared. When I moved, she moved with me. The man wasn't watching. I wanted to shout to him, *Hold on to this hand.* I wanted to tell him, *There's a boneyard in the woods, a hunter's pile of refuse, jaw of a beaver, vertebrae of a deer.* I wanted to tell him how easily we disappear.

That night I found Emile sleeping in a doorway. Shrunken little man with a white beard. No blanket, no coat. He opened one eye. *Cover me,* he said.

I held out my hands, empty palms, to show him all I had.

With your body, he said.

He held up his own hands, fingerless. *I froze once,* he said.

In the tunnel I found the Haitian man. Every time a train came, people tossed coins in his case and left him there. Still he sang, for me alone, left his ragged words flapping in my ribs.

Listen, the lungs float in water.

Listen, the lungs crackle in your hands.

Out of the body, the lungs simply collapse.

For my people, he said.

His skin was darker than mine, dark as my father's perhaps. His clothes grew bigger every day: he was singing himself sick. By February he'd be gone. By February I'd add the Haitian manchild to my list of the disappeared.

But that night I threw coins to him.

That night I believed in the miracles of wine and bread, how what we eat becomes our flesh.

It was almost Christmas. I put quarters in the phone to hear the words. *Come home if you want,* Adele said.

Clare made me remember the inside of the trailer. She made me count the beds. *Close the curtains — it's a box,* she said.

Clare made me see Adele at the table, the morning she told me she was going to marry Mick. *It's my last chance,* my mother said. I wanted the plates to fly out of the cupboard. I wanted to shatter every glass.

I smoked a cigarette instead.

I was thirteen.

It was ten A.M.

I drank a beer.

I felt sorry for Adele, I swear. She was thirty-four, an old woman with red hair. She said, *Look at me,* and I did, at her too-pale freckled skin going slack.

I thought, How many men can pass through one woman? I thought, How many children can one woman have? I tried to count: Clare's father and Clare, my father and me, two men between, two children never born whose tiny fingers still dug somewhere. She didn't need to make the words, *I feel them;*

didn't need to touch her body, *here*. I knew everything. It was her hand reaching for the cigarettes. It was the way she had to keep striking the match to get it lit. It was the color of her nails — pink, chipped.

If she'd been anyone but my mother I would have forgiven her for what she said.

I can't do it again. She meant she had another one on the way. She meant she couldn't make it end. So Mick was coming here, to live, bringing his already ten-year-old son, child of his dead first wife; the boy needed a mother, God knows, and I saw exactly how it would be with all of them, Mick and the boy and the baby — I could hear the wailing already, the unborn child weeping through my mother's flesh.

Clare made me remember all this. Clare made me hang up before my mother said the words *come home* again.

Storm that night, snow blown to two-foot drifts; rain froze them hard. *Forever*, Clare said.

She didn't know which needle, didn't know whose blood made her like this. She didn't know whose dangerous breath blew through her in the end. She told me she had a dream. We were alone in the trailer. Our little hands cast shadows on the wall: rabbit, bird, devil's head. She said, *Someone's hand passed over my lungs like that.*

I wanted to go home. I didn't care what she said. I saw the trailer in the distance, the colored lights blinking on and off, the miles of snow between me and them. I saw the shape of my mother move beyond curtain and glass.

It's too late to knock, Clare said.

She made me remember our first theft, Adele's car, all the windows down, made me see her at fifteen, myself at ten. We weren't running away: we were feeling the wind. We drove north, out of the dusty August day into the surprising twilight. I remember the blue of that sky, dark and brilliant, dense, like liquid, cool on our skin. And then ahead of us, glowing in a field, we saw a carnival tent, lit from inside.

Freaks, we thought, and we wanted to see, imagined we'd find the midget sisters, thirty-three inches high; the two-headed pig; the three-hundred-pound calf.

We wanted to see Don Juan the Dwarf, that silk robe, that black mustache. We wanted to buy his kisses for dimes. We wanted him to touch our faces with his stubby hands.

We wanted the tattooed woman to open her shirt. Pink-eyed albino lady. We wanted her to show us the birds of paradise on her old white chest.

We wanted to go into the final room, the draped booth at the far corner of the tent, we wanted to pay our extra dollar to see the babies in their jars: the one with half a brain and the twins joined hip to chest. We wanted to see our own faces reflected in that glass, to know our own bodies, revealed like this.

We wanted freaks, the strange thrill of them.

But this is what we found instead: ordinary cripples, a man in a violet robe promising Jesus would heal them.

We found children in wheelchairs. We saw their trembling limbs.

We saw a bald girl in a yellow dress.

We saw two boys with withered bodies and huge heads.

We saw all the mothers on their knees. We thought their cries would lift this tent.

Busted driving home. Adele knew who had the car but turned us in. *That's why I left,* Clare said.

I'm waiting for you on the road.

You could be anyone: a woman with a blond child, or the man in the blue truck come back. You could be the one who wants me dead. We meet at last.

I'm not trying to go home. I'm heading north instead.

Clare's tired. Clare's not talking now. If you're dangerous, I don't think she'll tell me.

I see swirling snow, pink light between bare trees, your car in the distance, moving fast. I speak out loud to hear myself. *Clare's gone,* I say. But when you spot me, when you swerve and stop, she surprises me. She says, *Go, little sister, get in.*

She whispers, *Yes, this is the one.*

I don't know what she means.

If you ask me where I want to go, I'll tell you this: *Take me out of the snow. Take me to a tent in a field. Make it summer. Make the sky too blue. Make the wind blow. Let me stand here with all the crippled children. Give me twisted bones and metal braces. Give me crutches so I can walk. Let my mother fall down weeping, begging the man in violet robes to make me whole.*

T H E

S N O W

T H I E F

/// MY FATHER FLED without waking. Snow fell. The ghost of an elk drifted between trees. Mother called that November morning. *Gone,* she said, as if he might be missing. He was sixty-nine, still quick and wiry, a tow-truck driver who cruised county roads rescuing women like me.

A single vessel ruptures; blood billows in the brain. That fast. Impossible to believe. Eleven years since he'd caught me with his friend Jack Fetters in the back seat. No one could blame his bursting artery on me. No one except my father himself. He filled my one-room flat on Water Street. I smelled smoke in damp wool, saw the shadow of his hand pass close to my face.

Simply dead. How could this be? He'd wounded the elk at dawn, tracked it for miles down the ravine. Near dark, the bull became an owl and flew away.

Lungs freeze. Hearts fail. It's easy. I know it happens everywhere, hundreds of times a day, to daughters much younger than I was then. Still, each one leaves a mystery.

As my father slipped into bed that night, he said, *My shoulder hurts. Could you rub me?*

And Mother whispered, *I'm too sleepy.*

It drove her mad. Over and over she said the same thing: *I was going to rub his shoulder in the morning.*

I thought we'd lose her. She kept asking, *How could I sleep with your father dead beside me?* I remember how suddenly she shrank, how nothing she ate stayed with her. My brother wanted to put her away. *A home,* Wayne said, *for her own safety.*

One night we found all her windows open, the back door flapping. We caught her three miles up the highway. She stood in the middle of the road, as if she'd felt us coming and had paused to wait. Our headlights blasted through worn cloth, revealed small drooping breasts and tense legs, bare feet too cold to bleed. She wore only her tattered nightgown. No underpants beneath it. Nothing.

She wouldn't ride in the truck. I gave her my coat and boots. I wore Wayne's. He had to drive in stocking feet. Mother and I walked together, silent the whole way. I held her arm to keep her steady. But this is the truth: she was the one to steady me. It made sense, this cold — a kind of prayer, this ceaseless walking.

When we got home, she let me wash her feet. I told her she was lucky, no frostbite, and she said, *Lucky?*

Then she slept, fifty-six hours straight.

The doctor said, *She needs this. She's healing.*

I washed her whole body. She hadn't bathed for twelve days. My mother, that smell! Air too thick to breathe, tight as skin around me.

She woke wanting sausages and steak. Eggs fried in bacon grease. A can of hash with corned beef. She ate like this for days and days, stayed skinny all the same. *It's your father,* she said. *He's hungry.*

He took her piece by piece. For thirteen years my mother stumbled in tracks she couldn't see. Every year another stroke left another tiny hole in her brain. I thought of it this way, saw our father standing at the edge of the pines, his gun raised. He was firing at Mother; but it was dusk, and since he was dead, his aim was unsteady. Each time he hit, she staggered toward him. He was a proud man, even now. It was his way of calling.

In the end, he defeated himself. All those scars left spaces empty. She forgot why she'd gone to the woods and who she wanted to find there. She loved only her nurse, and almost forgot my father, and almost forgot my brother and me.

I caught the pretty boy smoothing her sheet. Thin as an angel, this Rafael, so graceful he seemed to be dancing. He held her wrist to feel the pulse. He checked her IV. He said, *What a beautiful way to eat.*

He loved her too. How can anyone explain? He wasn't afraid of burned thighs or skin peeling. He touched her feathery hair, sparse and fine as wet down on one of the unborn chicks my brother kept in jars of formaldehyde the year he was fourteen. Specimens, he called them, his eighth-grade science project. Every two days he cracked another egg to examine the fetus. I hated myself, remembering this, seeing my own mother curl up like one of these. But there they were, those jars of yellow fluid, those creatures floating.

I stroked her arm to make her wake.
What do you want now? she said.
To say goodnight.
Not goodbye?
Not yet.
It's not up to you, she said. She was seventy-seven years old, seventy-three pounds the last time anyone checked.
What did I want?
I wanted her big again. Tall as my father. Wide in the hips.
Think of me as a child. Once, when I was sick, my mother

sat three days beside me, afraid to sleep because I might stop breathing. Sometimes when I woke I smelled deerskin and tobacco, felt my father's cool hand on my forehead.

I have this proof they loved me.

What went wrong?

I turned fifteen. Jack Fetters said, *Someday, Marie.* Jack Fetters whispered, *We're not so different as you think.*

He was a guard at the state penitentiary. He said, *Man goes crazy watching other men all day.* His wife, Edie, had some terrible disease with a jungle name. Made her arms and legs puff up huge, three times their normal size. Jack Fetters said, *Sometimes the body is a cage.* They had a little girl just five, another seventeen, four boys in the middle. The one I knew had found his profession already: Nate Fetters was a sixteen-year-old car thief.

I thought, sooner or later his own daddy and a pack of dogs will chase him up a tree. Would Jack Fetters haul his son back to town, or would he chain the animals and let the thief escape?

A trap, either way.

I liked that boy, Nate Fetters. But he never noticed me. It was the father who touched my neck under my hair. It was the father I slapped away. The father who kept finding me. After school, at the edge of town, throwing rocks down the ravine. The patient father. *Someday, Marie.*

Was he handsome?

How can I explain?

He was the wolfman in a dream, a shape-shifter, caught halfway between what he was and what he was going to be. Even before I unbuttoned his shirt, I imagined silvery fur along his spine. Before I pulled his pants to his ankles, I saw his skinny wolf legs. I knew he'd grunt and moan on top of me. Bite too hard. Come too quickly.

This part I didn't see: a car pulled off the road, a back seat — my father with a flashlight, breaking glass above me. I never guessed my own belly would swell up huge like Edie's legs.

Wayne sat on the window ledge. Our mother's room. Another day.

She's worse, he said.

At last, I thought, it's ending.

But he didn't mean this.

He said, *She promised that little fairy her damn TV.*

I knew Wayne. He wanted the color television. He figured he'd earned it, living with Mother. Thirteen years. *I've done my time.* That's what he'd say.

Her eyelids fluttered. She was asking God, *What did I do to deserve children like these?*

Listen, I felt sorry for my brother. He was soon to be an orphan. Just like me.

Once we hid in the ravine, that dangerous place, forbidden, where fugitives dug caves, where terrified girls changed themselves to pine trees. We buried ourselves under dirt and damp leaves. We couldn't speak or see. We couldn't *be* seen. God only glanced our way. If he saw the pile of leaves, he thought it was his wind rustling. He turned his gaze. He let us do it. He let us slip our little hands under each other's clothes. Warm hands. So small! Child hands. So much the same. God didn't thunder in our ears. God didn't hurl his lightning.

But later he must have guessed. He came as brittle light between black branches. He was each one blaming the other.

He showed himself as blindness, the path through trees suddenly overgrown with thorns and briars. He came as fear. He turned to root and stone to trip us.

The man on my mother's window ledge had split knuckles, a stubbled beard, bloated face. He said, *It's late. I work tonight.* He said, *Call me if there's any change.*

First love gone to this. If I said, *Remember?*, Wayne would say I'd had a dream. He'd say I was a scrawny brat. He'd say the closest thing he ever gave me to a kiss was a rope burn around my wrist.

This is how God gets revenge: he leaves one to remember and one to forget.

The boy I loved had been struck dead.

At twenty, Wayne said, *This whole town is a penitentiary.* He meant to climb the wall and leap. No barbed wire. No snags. He moved up and down the coast, Anchorage to Los Angeles. He wrote once a year. Every time he was just about to make some real money. But after our father died, Wayne came home to Mother, safe, took a job with Esther McQuade at the 4-Doors Bar on Main Street. *It's a good business,* he said. *Everybody has to drink.*

Six months later, he married Esther's pregnant daughter. Some kind of trade. He said, *I know this first one's not gonna look much like me.* Now he was Esther's partner instead of her employee.

But he was still jealous, thought I must be smart and lucky. Because I went to college, two years. Because I got as far as Missoula and stayed. Eighty miles. I wanted to tell him, *No matter where I go, I'm just the same.*

Did he blame himself for Mother's last accident?

I never asked. I knew what he'd say. *Just because she lives in my house doesn't mean I trot to the bathroom with her.*

She spent two days in bed before she told him. A tub of scalding water, thighs and buttocks burning. She was ashamed. *I just sat down,* she said. *I wasn't thinking.*

By the time she showed him, the skin was raw, the wounds infected. She couldn't ride a single mile. The doctor who came to the house gave her morphine. He said, *How did you stand it?*

And she said, *I forgot my body.*

This doctor was a boy, blinking behind thick glasses. He couldn't grasp her meaning. Mother said, *Go ask your father. Maybe he can tell you.*

The doctor shook his head. No way to help her here in Deer Lodge. He said, *We'll have to fly you to Missoula.*

Yes, she said, *I'd like that.* She meant the ride, the helicopter.

Now this, three weeks of antibiotics and painkillers pumped into veins that kept collapsing. She had a doctor for each part of her: one for skin and one for brain, one to save her from pneumonia. But all of them together couldn't heal her whole body. The neurologist rubbed his clean hands as if they hurt him. He stood near the window — gray light, white jacket, all I remember. He tried to explain it. *Common with stroke victims, immune system impaired, the body can't fight infection.* He said, *It's one thing after another, like stomping out brush fires.*

We were alone at last. I smoothed her hair. She curled into herself, tiny bird of a woman, still shrinking, becoming my child, my unborn mother. I leaned close to whisper. *It's me,* I said, *Marie, your daughter.*

Rain hit the glass. Then Rafael appeared, off-duty, wearing his black coat draped around his shoulders. He washed her face. He said, *She likes this. See? She's smiling.* He said, *Go home if you're tired. I can stay awhile.*

His coat was frayed, not warm, not good in rain. Maybe he had nowhere else to go. No house, no room, no bed, no lover. Maybe this was the reason for his kindness. Who can know our secrets?

I saw my father in the parking lot, gun propped against a dumpster. He searched his pockets. Found no bullets. He knew Rafael was with my mother. So close at last, and he'd lost her all the same.

I meant to go home and bolt the door. But rain turned to sleet, sent me spinning. One wrong turn and I found myself at the Bearpaw Bar on Evaro.

Animals hung. Buffalo, moose, grizzly. This last one had its hide attached. I thought their bodies must be trapped behind these walls. I told the man beside me I'd break them free if I had a pick and axe. He had pointy teeth, a glad-dog grin. He said, *Where were you when they locked me down in Deer Lodge?* His skin was cracked, a Badlands face. When he smiled that way, I was afraid the scars might split open. This Tully bought my third beer, my first bourbon. He gripped my knee. He said, *I like you.*

By the jukebox, two sisters swayed, eyes closed, mouths moving. Sleepdancers. My father leaned against the wall, watching their smooth faces and the dreamy tilt of their hips rolling. I passed him on my way to the bathroom. His coat was wet. I smelled metal and oil, a gun just cleaned, grease on his fingers.

Too many beers already. I knew how it would be, how I'd follow Tully to the Easy Sleep Motel, take off my clothes too fast to think.

But when I saw my father, I had hope I could be saved. I thought, *I won't do this if you'll talk to me.* I said his name. I whispered, *Daddy?*

He didn't hear. Deaf old man. He looked away.

Listen.

They never brought my son to me. They let me sob, sore and swollen. They let my breasts bleed milk for days.

In every room another girl, just the same. In every room the calm Catholic women said, *Gone, a good family.*

Listen. There were complications. Narrow pelvis, fetus turned the wrong way. They had to cut my child out of me. Days later, they cut again.

Infection, the doctor said. *It has to drain.*

One slip of the knife. And a girl becomes a childless mother forever. It's easy. The good women promised, *No more accidents.* Between themselves they murmured, *It's a blessing.*

Listen.

No father lets you tell him this.

In the bathroom, I tried to see myself, but I wasn't there. I was black eyebrows and lipstick smeared. The rest of me was hidden, inside the wavy glass. I imagined opening a door, falling on a bed. I saw the marks my mouth would leave, bright blooms on scarred flesh. I saw a spiderweb tattooed on Tully's hairless chest.

What did I care if some old man judged me?

Listen. I'm snow in wind. No one leaves his imprint.

I went back to the bar, another beer, a third bourbon. Tully's hand moved up my leg. I'd hit black ice, locked my tires in a skid.

And then, a miracle, an angel sweet as Rafael sent to rescue stranded women. God spit him from the mouth of the buffalo head. Skinny boy in black jeans and leather. He pulled me off my stool. He said, *Maybe we should dance.*

The old man shot coins into the jukebox. My friend, after all. They were in this together, partners, a father and son with a tow truck, saviors with a hook and winch sent to pull me from the ditch.

Those thick-thighed sisters took care of Tully. One lit his cigarette, one stuck her tongue in his ear. They'd fallen with the snow, melted in my hair. They were my strange twins, myself grown fat. Their nails were long and hard, their lips a blazing red. Angels, both of them. You never know how they'll appear.

That boy's big hands were on my back. He whirled me in a dip and spin. His leg slipped between my legs.

What are we doing? I asked.

Only dancing, he said.

Yes, dancing. There's no harm in it. But later it was more a droop and drag, a slow waltz, one of us too drunk to stand.

The old man sat at a table in the back, holding his head in his hands. I saw how wrong I'd been. No angels here. The scarred man and the twins left. I was alone, reeling with the boy called Dez.

He ran his hands along my hips, pressed me into him. I said, *You're young enough to be my kid.*

But I'm not, he said.

He wrapped his fingers around my neck. He said, *Listen, baby, I'm low on cash.*

One last chance. I bought my freedom, gave him fifty-two dollars, all I had. He stuck it down his boot. I thought he'd vanish then, blow out the door, a swirl of smoke. But he said, *Let's go outside. This cowboy's got to get some air.*

In my car, he kissed me in that stupid way, all tongue and no breath. I lost my head. Then we were driving somewhere, snow-blind, no seatbelts, nothing to strap us in. I saw broken glass, our bright bodies flying into tiny bits.

I took him home. Who can explain this? His long hair smelled of mud. I found damp leaves hidden in his pockets. His palms were cool on my forehead. He opened me. With his tongue, he traced the scar across my belly. It was wet and new. In a room years away I heard a child crying.

I expected him to steal everything. He touched the bones of my pelvis as if remembering the parts of me, veins of my hands, sockets of my eyes. *Like a sister,* he said. I thought he whispered *Darling* just before we slept.

In the morning he disappeared. Took my sleeping bag and cigarettes.

Then the phone rang and a voice said, *Your mother, gone.* Imagine.

Everyone you love is missing. The voice on the phone never tells me this. The voice says, *Body, arrangements.* The voice says, *Your brother's on his way. You can meet him here.* I don't argue. I say, *Yes.* But I don't go to the hospital. I know I'll never catch them there.

Hours gone. *While you danced. While you lay naked in your bed.* That's what the voice in my own skull says.

I go to the ravine where the wounded elk staggers between pines. It's always November here, always snowing. It's the night my father died. It's the morning my mother is dying.

Sky is gray, snow fills it. Trees bend with ice, limbs heavy. I climb down, no tracks to follow. Snow higher than my boots already, a cold I hardly notice. I forget my body. How will I find them if they don't want me?

Flakes cluster, the size of children's palms now. They break against my head and back, so light I cannot feel them. I glimpse shapes, trees in wind shifting, clumps of snow blown from them, big as men's fists, big as stones falling. They burst. Silent bombs, scattering fragments.

Nothing nothing happens. Nothing hurts me.

And then I see them. He's wearing his plaid coat and wool pants, a red cap with earflaps. She wears only her pink night-gown. He carries her. She's thin as a child but still a burden, and the snow is deep, and I see how he struggles. I could call out, but they'll never hear me. I can't speak in these woods. A shout would make the sky crumble. All the snow that ever was would bury me.

Deeper and deeper, the snow, the ravine. He never slows his pace. He never turns to look for me. Old man, slumped shoulders. All I ever wanted was to touch him, his body, so he could heal me, with his hair and bones, the way a saint heals. I hear my own breath. I stumble. How does he keep going?

Now I climb the steep slope. With every step I'm slipping. The distance between them and me keeps growing. I know I'll lose them. I know the place it happens. I know the hour. Dusk, the edge of the woods. The white elk takes flight as an owl in absolute silence. Wings open a hole in the sky, and a man and a woman walk through it.

No one says, *Go back.* No one says, *You'll die here.* But the cold, I feel it. My own body, I'm back in it.

I can stay. I can lie down. Let the snow fall on my face. Let its hands be tender.

Or I can walk, try to find my way in darkness.

I'm a grown woman, an orphan, I have these choices.

B O D I E S

O F

W A T E R

/// ELENA SEES HERSELF as the boy did: a woman on the Ave., alone in the U District. It's late afternoon, January. He's hunched in a doorway. After a half-hour watching women, he chooses her. She's the one in the red raincoat, easy to track, light-boned and skittery.

He strikes hard, punches her left kidney. Slits the strap of her purse. Kicks the backs of her legs.

She twists, staggered; glimpses a boy in a black jacket sprinting down an alley.

Someone touches her shoulder.

Someone asks, *Are you okay?*

Elena's on her knees. She feels little hands still pressed against her ribs. Short fingers. Wide palms. He's a tough boy. She remembers the extra push, the second kick. He wants her down. He leaves her there.

This is the bridge on the West Seattle Freeway.

The only way home.

Elena's stuck in traffic. There's been an accident again, third time this month: another car crushed into the guardrail, another woman standing stunned in the rain.

Home at last but not safe, Elena Brissard doesn't tell her husband about the accident or the thief. He's too comfortable, listening to the cheerful flutes of his Vivaldi. Eating olives, drinking Tanqueray.

And she doesn't tell her daughter.

Iris lies on the bed in her basement room, dead poet crying in her skull. She loves him above all others, this wailing boy who pulled his own trigger: heroin first to ease the passage, shotgun to be sure. Through the windows of his greenhouse, he watched clouds and mountains grow very small.

Elena's guessing. Iris uses headphones, always, so the bitter riffs of his guitar are only vibrations buzzing in the kitchen floor.

Elena flicks the light on the stairs and waits in the hallway. These are the rules. She's forbidden to enter her daughter's room or knock too loudly.

Iris lifts one headphone.

Is she hungry?

No, never mind.

She'd rather stay here, with him, than sit at the table with Elena and Geoffrey. Elena doesn't know why she keeps inviting. Iris is the hunger artist. She hasn't eaten with them since she disappeared for eight days last July. Not stolen. She ran away. *These kids just vanish,* the policeman told them. *Fall into cracks in the street.* He wasn't trying to be cruel. He said there was a jungle under I-5, tents and shacks hidden in trees, a city beneath the city. *You want my advice?* he said. *Pray.*

Elena lights tapers while Geoffrey pops the cork on a bottle of pouilly-fuissé. A boy looking through these windows could mistake them for lovers. They eat cold salmon dipped in hollandaise. Pale green hearts of artichokes. Brilliant raspberries.

So polite, husband and wife, each asking, *How was your day?* He's gotten a shipment from Cape Dorset: musk ox and caribou, whales scooped from whalebone, a green owl carved by a blind man who listens to the stones until they speak their shapes. Geoffrey says, *A perfect piece — you have to close your eyes to see its wings.* But Elena knows it's old work he loves most, yellowed ivory: a hermaphrodite with walrus tusks, a bear with six legs. The Inuit say, *There are things in nature man must not explain.* He can't sell these. They belong in museums. Behind glass. Safe. He stuffs them in socks or rolls them in pillowcases. His rooms are full of strange creatures. Open any box in any closet and you'll find one, wrapped like a little mummy.

How can Elena judge him? She lives in his house on the hill. Drives his blue Mazda. Drinks his Courvoisier.

There should be bars on these windows. That's what Iris says. Iris says, *You're a hostage — just like me.*

The boy who snatched Elena's purse is fifty-seven dollars richer tonight and still soaked, still shivering, looking for a place to sleep. But tonight, thanks to Elena, he's not hungry. He's gorged himself: three burgers, a chocolate milkshake. He can smoke all he wants, one cigarette after another, no rationing. He has money for a second pack and a third one in the morning. *Tonight,* Elena thinks, *he almost forgives me.*

This is the totem pole, Pioneer Square, two days later: raven and otter squat one on top of the other, mindless in the wind and rain.

No wild children here, just trembling men with broken teeth. They have hands like Elena's father's. Unsteady. They drink from bottles in paper bags. Leave green glass splintered in the street.

Elena sips cappuccino in a warm café. *Three-dollar cup of foam.* That's what Iris would say. Iris makes her want to leave this place.

Outside, they're starving.

Outside, the sky's gone yellow.

Elena leans into the wind because she lacks weight. In every stoop she sees an old man's face.

Do the men with cracked skin care how she wastes her money? No. Do they sputter or beg? No. They murmur. Three dollars. Nothing.

Then she spots him, the boy again, her little thief. He's found her already, miles from the Ave., here at the other end of the city.

Not him, but one like him.

Just another boy wearing a hooded sweatshirt under a black jacket.

He crouches in a cul-de-sac. Drenched. He's been expecting her. He grins. *Yes, it's me,* he says. Not out loud. Not in a way that anyone besides Elena hears. Tiny hands slip through her ribcage. Wind blows through her chest.

They hate us.

All these lost kids.

She walks fast. Cars spray water from her ankles to her neck. She catches her own reflection in wavy glass, listens to her own heels click on cement.

At the car, she sees how stupid she's been. Her door, unlocked. She's asking for it. Years ago, before Geoff, there were boys in her father's orchard, brown hands on white wrists. Their tongues in her mouth were the only words they shared.

She married Geoff to stop all that. Her dangerous self-forgetting. Her accidents.

Now that smell is in her car. Smoke and spit, something damp and too familiar, the leaves where she lay down, played dead. She's afraid to check the back seat or glance in the rearview mirror. If she looks, she thinks she'll conjure one of them. Fruit picker's son. *Migrant.* Her father told her he'd throttle any daughter he caught with one of them. *Throttle.* When he said the word, his hands in air gripped an imaginary neck.

Elena's home again. That safe house on the hill.

The boy's across the water, trapped on the other side of the bridge. No one can touch her. No father will call to curse or raise his fist. She chooses when to go to him. Poor old man, lost in his own front yard. Kind nurses lead him to his door again and again. *Where's Esther?* he says. He forgets his wife is dead. Sometimes he calls and calls, then weeps when she won't answer him. He thinks three nurses who come in shifts are all the same man. They have skin murky as nights in the orchard. You could disappear in them. Daddy's nurses have big thighs, thick chests. *The better to lift you, my dear.* Her father's thin but still heavy. She imagines bowels full of stones, Daddy digging rocks, eating fast. The nurses call him Baby. Cut his meat in tiny bits. Change his soiled pants.

If you wait long enough, everyone you fear will come to this.

Elena stares out the window, watching green clouds scud and swell. Two messages on the machine. Geoffrey says he's working late. *Sorry, sweetheart.* Iris says, *My ride split.* She might be stranded, might sleep in a shelter on the Ave. This is as kind as Iris gets. She means, *Don't worry. I'm not down in the jungle yet.*

Waves of rain break hard on glass. Elena runs from room to room, popping lights, rolling towels along the sills, but the rain has no heart, no shape it has to keep, no head — the rain flows through every crack. She wants Iris to call again. *Please come.* She'd go anywhere. *Yes, even in this.* When the phone rings at last, it's only Geoff. He can't get home. *Pileup on the bridge.* He'll have to sleep at the office. He says, *I'll call you back.*

But this never happens.

An hour later the whole hill goes dark; the phone goes dead.

Now it's Elena and the storm. The two of them. She torches last night's candles. Shadows jump against the walls. Elena's jittery hand. Elena's own head. She hasn't eaten all day. She could make hot chocolate. The stove's gas. She pours two shots of Chivas in her mug instead.

Windows flex and clatter. The house throbs with her body: she's the pounding heart in it. Shrubs scritch and slap. Limbs snap. Limbs tear. She thinks of the men from the square, wonders if they crawled into dumpsters and closed the lids.

Somewhere a door slams. Iris blown home? This is Elena's prayer. In the kitchen, the back screen flaps. When she tries to latch it, a gust rips it from her hands. Hinges shear. Pellets hit her face, icy rain, tiny stones tossed by a tiny fist. The boy, she thinks, he's out there. Voices roar in the whirlwind, all the lost children rising out of mud and grass.

Is she drunk already? Skinny woman, empty stomach — she tells herself that's all it is.

Another door bangs below her, the one from garage to basement. *Please, God, make it Iris.* She stands at the top of the stairs and calls. No answer, only that smell of feral cat.

She takes her bottle to the couch, doesn't bother with the mug. Candles gutter and flare. The animal follows, marks its territory, sprays its scent. She feels it heave in the leather beneath her thighs and back. Someone's sewn its torn chest. Someone's filled its belly with blood and gas.

She drifts. Dreams the creature on top of her. Crushing air from her lungs. Pinching veins in her neck. This beast has a thick hide and six hands. He's heavy as three men. Feathers slap her face. Then it's only the boy. Small, hard. The one from the Ave. The one from the square. The child. Little fingers too short to grip her neck. But he has his knife. And he's so fast.

Then it's Iris. White face, purple mouth. Iris with her sharp hips. Shaking her wet hair. Iris so close they take the same breath. Iris says, *You know why I came back?*

She jolts awake. Alone. It's her own body that makes the couch warm. Her sweat. It's her own small fist shoved in her mouth. Her own will that keeps her silent.

In the kitchen, a simple click. The refrigerator door opened and closed. Could it be that harmless? Iris willing to eat her food at last? No. Iris drinks coffee with cream. Eats salsa and chips. Once a day. Never here. The one in the kitchen cracks four eggs in a quart of milk, shakes three times, guzzles it. He tears off chunks of sausage with his pointy teeth. *The better to eat you,* he says.

Please, she thinks, make it quick. She remembers all those forbidden boys — black hair, dirty hands — Mexicans who picked fruit in her father's orchards; Indians who worked for nobody, who never would, that's what her father said; almost blue boys who sat on mailboxes, who pretended not to see the girl hiding in her pale skin, who said things she couldn't understand as she passed, low things, tender threats, murmurs that made her feel flushed and damp, curses that made her want to beg forgiveness. *I'll throttle you. If I ever catch you with a boy like that.* So she was with the clean white boys in the field. Drinking rum. And it was dark. And there was no color anywhere. So it was safe. And they were nice boys, sons of her father's friends, boys she'd known since kindergarten, boys who were going to college next year. So how could she explain their hands on her, the marks they left, fingerprints on soft flesh, green bruises, arms gripped? How could she explain red marks on her neck and breasts? How could she go home and who could she blame and who would her father throttle if she confessed?

Later she thought she made it up. Just a bad dream, a hot wind full of dust. The next night she sat at the dinner table, moving her fork to her mouth, chewing, swallowing, as if eating still made sense.

Where was Mother?

In the bathroom with the door locked, lying in the tub, water so deep she could float.

Where was Little Sister?

In the kitchen getting Daddy another scotch and milk.

Years later little Julie was the one. Just like Elena. High in the parched hills above Yakima. Laughing, drunk. Then she was crying, clawing at the ground.

No one's ever going to hear her.

No one's ever going to come.

These sisters keep their silence forever. Each pretending the other doesn't know.

How did Elena guess? She sat awake all night watching shooting stars flame out. Near dawn, Little Sister climbed in the window down the hall. Elena heard the shower pound and pound; she remembered her own skin, imagined Julie naked, scrubbing herself raw till scalding water ran ice cold.

Tonight Elena lies in another house, safe from her sister's voice, deaf to words never said out loud: *If you knew, why didn't you help?* How many years since Julie climbed in that window? Decades now. How many months since they've spoken on the phone? Elena can't remember, doesn't want to count. Julie has three ex-husbands and four children lost. The last time she called, Julie said the kids were still in foster care but she'd gotten sober, found God.

This time it's not her sister sneaking in the window. Not her sister rattling doors in this house.

It's the boy. She's sure. Wet dog. The smell in the back seat all along. *Yes, you brought him here yourself.*

She crawls. She still has this advantage. It's her house. She knows its obstacles. She scrambles to the stairs, where she can close one more door, slide one more bolt.

She can trap herself. Lie down in the tub. Roll under the bed. Squat in the closet.

She can make herself very small.

She can slip into Geoffrey's suit and shoes, pretend to be someone else. She can plead for mercy, make bargains, talk to Julie's God. She can swear she'll never tell. *I forget your face already.*

She can say, *Take anything you want.*

The boy roars with laughter.

He says, *Thanks, I will.*

His voice fills her lungs like God. He holds all the cards. He has no reason to make deals with stupid girls.

But what does he want with her body? And what will he do with her blood?

This is where she finally goes: into the attic under the eaves, the coldest place, the cobwebbed peak of the house. It's the last place he'll look. Birds flap against a tiny window. Pigeons, swallows, gulls. They tap, all beak and claw. She could save them, cover her fist to break a hole. But she's afraid they've gone mad in the storm. Afraid they'll peck her apart.

There's a trunk half full of sweaters where she lies down, deep in the smell of cedar, wrapped in Mother's frayed quilt.

She hopes the boy finds the bottle of Chivas by the couch and drinks it all. She hopes he finds Geoffrey's Goldschläger, twenty-four-karat flakes swirling in schnapps. She dreams veins full of metal, heart clogged with gold. She imagines morning, finding the boy curled on the floor, kneeling beside him, tying him with twine and scarves. She'll wait for him to wake. She'll say, *Let me take you home.*

The house erupts. The boy hears this thought. *Home.* His voice is exploding glass, a tree limb torn.

He says, *I had a mother once, stupid as you are now.*

The boy says, *I have names, things people call me, words my mother gave me — my father's name, as if she always planned to throw me out.*

Boys call me one thing.

Girls call me another.

But in my head I say these names: Ice, Mud, River.

I have enemies: the kid who owned this jacket, the rain tonight, my own memory.

Don't touch me when I'm sleeping.

I hate fingers in my hair, fat women, the smell of baby powder.

I have a knife inside a secret pocket.

Surprise me and I'll kill you.

I need gloves, a blanket, a place to lie down, a hole to hide me.

I don't like birds. They scare me. All that noise. Their hunger. They remind me that I'm hungry.

I don't like dogs. They make me bark. They make me want to bite them.

I killed a cat once. Not on purpose. But later I wasn't sorry. It startled me, my hands around it, the way it twitched, the way it stopped twitching.

Mostly I hate pigeons, rats with wings — and squirrels, rats with bushy tails.

When I'm alone, I hate the sound in my own veins, the way it fills the room, like God whispering.

I love the dark, the sewer, the closet — all the places I'm invisible.

I love the water when it's deep and wants to drown me.

I love the bottle in my hand, green glass, jagged edges. I love my cut palms, warm blood when it turns thick as pudding.

I love the bridge when the wind is cold and I'm almost jumping.

I love your house, the way locks burst and doors open.

I love the smell of rum and chocolate, my sticky fingers.

I love these walls so much I leave my handprints.

Am I really here?

I am if you believe it.

I love the way I scare you, the way my heart becomes your heart, the way our pulse surges.

The boy cries at every door, *Mother.* Elena remembers Iris shut in the upstairs bedroom. Iris wailing. She remembers hiding in the basement, in the bathroom, with the water drumming.

So I wouldn't hear her.

She was afraid of her own daughter, two months old, Iris whimpering. She was afraid of tiny arms and fragile fingers. Afraid of herself, what she might do to stop this squalling.

She locked all the doors between them.

The boy howls. He knows this. He says, *Put your hand on my head, feel how flat the back is.*

Yes, she understands. If you leave a child long enough, the soft bones of the skull will flatten.

He says, *No wonder we hate you.*

Elena whispers, *But that didn't happen.* Elena says, *Iris has a perfect head, a lovely curve — I didn't hurt her.*

The boy laughs. The boy says, *You think I don't know that?* The boy says, *You think I haven't touched her?*

He says, *She lived in the jungle eight days last summer. I remember her voice. She's sweet, your Iris. But mostly it's her throat I remember. So white I wanted to snap it. I wanted to lie down beside her with my eyes closed. I wanted to rub naked against her until her skin was sore and red and mine was healed.*

Why should I be me? Why should she be Iris?

One night she must have heard me. My thoughts. She must have dreamed the words inside me. The next day she disappeared. Came home. To you. To this house. Not because she loves you. Only because I scare her. She'll get over that. Don't think that you can keep her.

The boy says, *She told us where you live, how easy it would be to rob you.* He says, *When I saw you on the Ave. that day, I knew we were meant to be together.*

Elena wants to tell the boy, *Everybody suffers.* Wants to say that children who live in cars and children who live in castles sit awake all night watching stars, wondering why meteors don't set the earth on fire. Children everywhere wonder why their mothers refuse to answer. Children lie in the grass, waiting for fathers who never come to save them.

The boy is very practical. The boy says, *You sleep in the car. I'll sleep in the castle.* He says, *You eat from the dumpster. I'll eat your salmon and raspberries.* He says, *I'll lie under the down comforter. You can stuff your pants with newspaper.*

He says, *Maybe you're right.* He says, *Maybe I'll still suffer.* He says, *I'm willing to try it.*

He hasn't been this warm in years. He says, *I think I'd like to die here.* He says, *We die every night in the jungle. Last week it was a migrant. One of those fools who forgot to go south for the winter. He ended up with us instead, under the freeway, in a house made of sticks and cardboard. He was hacking yellow phlegm and bleeding from his asshole. Maybe you're right. When it comes to this, it doesn't matter if you're in the car or in the castle. On the white bed or the cold vinyl. But if I had my choice, I'd stay in your house forever.*

We didn't let him die in the dirt. We made a bed of leaves, wrapped our hands in rags to lift him. Someone covered him with a silver blanket. Our astronaut.

He asked us to find the sin-eater. Who knows how many of us there are? Ten thousand in this city? But we found her, the one he wanted, shriveled-up old spook of a woman. She came and sat beside him. Ate everything we brought her — boiled cat, raw fish, roasted squirrel. She swelled and swelled. Choked down his evil. Drank gallons of water. Belched and farted. She chewed till her eyes rolled and she toppled over. We thought his sins had killed her. All that meat, his poison. She slept two days. Foul. We had to tie shirts over our noses. The man burned. Riding that horse. No one could stop him. But his body wanted to stay with us. It breathed and bled. It snorted. Once its eyes opened.

On the third day, the sin-eater woke. Small again. Her withered self. Wind blew through the stick house. Rain washed us. We smelled like the ocean, salt and seaweed. We were clean, in a way, as clean as we can be. Our astronaut was wet and cool. His blanket shimmered like liquid silver. We wrapped it around him. A girl with little hands sewed it shut with tiny stitches.

That night we carried him to the highway and left him on the shoulder. We were too tired to dig a hole. And there are too many of us to bury. We could dig all day every day, turn this jungle to a graveyard.

If you leave a dead man on the road, someone always takes him.

He disappeared at daybreak.

We have this kind of magic.

When it was dark again, the silver blanket burst above me. A billion stars exploded. I was afraid. I thought it was his body breaking. If blood splattered in my eyes and mouth, I'd be the next one dying. But there were only stars and the black sky between them.

The boy is very tired. Too tired to keep talking. He whispers his last words to Elena. He says, *Every night ends if you live through it.*

This night does end. The rain is soft now. Elena climbs out of the trunk. She's not scared. She knows the boy has vanished.

Room by room, she'll find everything he's left her.

In her bed, she'll find his imprint. Everywhere he's been, he's carved a hole, a space for her to enter. Yes, it's true, when she touches the spot where his head lay on her pillow, she knows how flat his skull is. Between the sheets, she feels his short legs and curved clavicle, the three places where his arm was broken.

In the bathroom, she finds specks of blood in the sink, knows he tried to brush his teeth. His teeth are stained, his gums infected. He defines himself by absence, by what he's taken: three bars of soap, toothpaste and toothbrush, a box of Band-Aids. He's left a ring of scum in the tub, two wet towels, a damp bathmat. She finds blood here too. The boy scraped his flesh this hard and still felt filthy.

On the kitchen counter, she finds four eggshells, spilled milk, the empty carton. He's taken a tin of cashews and a box of powdered chocolate.

In the dining room, she finds shattered glasses, her favorite ones, hand-blown in Murano. She sees the broken window. No birds have flown inside her house, but in the shards she hears trapped cries and torn wings quivering.

The boy's pulled ivory creatures from the closet: an otter swallowing a lynx, a wolf mounting a caribou. Strange couplings. He has no use for these, and so he leaves them.

She follows him downstairs, his trail of sticky handprints. This is where he's strongest, where he was in the beginning and where he was in the end. Before he came upstairs, he must have lain on Iris's bed with his shoes on. He changed his clothes here. He's left his dirty pants, his hooded sweatshirt. Elena imagines what he's wearing now. Iris's ripped jeans, Geoffrey's leather jacket. He has her black alpaca sweater. She remembers an open drawer upstairs, thinks he took a pair of stockings. Practical boy. Will he wear them under the jeans, stay warm this winter? No, he'd never do that. He'll pull one leg of her pantyhose over his face to smash his nose and lips flat. No one will recognize him. Except Elena. *Yes,* she thinks, *I know the curved bones of your shoulders. The silt under your nails. I know the texture of your hair between my fingers. I know you as I know my own child, as I know myself, as I know my sister.*

She takes his little pile of clothes to the trash can. The rain is cold, a fine drizzle. She smells split wood, fresh sap, grass shredded. Out here there's no scent of boy to follow.

She tugs the sheets and comforter from Iris's bed. When the electricity comes back on, she'll wash them. She wipes fingerprints from the wall, throws out eggshells. Scours sink and bathtub. Smoothes pillowcases. She erases him. She has to. No one would understand. No one would believe her. Just a drunk woman throwing her own glasses. A scared, silly woman hiding in the attic. She presses her face to the pillow, wondering how many days she'll breathe him.

This morning her husband will come home and find her weeping. She won't explain this.

Tonight her daughter will appear, as if by magic. Thin, wet Iris. Slender stalk of her body in dark clothes, white bloom of her face. Iris in the doorway. Lighting a cigarette. Iris saying, *Mind if I smoke here?*

Tonight Elena will lie down beside her husband. If he touches thigh or cheek, she'll tell him she's exhausted. When he drops off at last, she'll go down the basement stairs to watch her daughter. She'll stay almost an hour, hoping Iris won't wake and see her. Hoping Iris won't say, *What are you doing?*

Later she'll sit beside an open window to watch the rain, knowing that behind those clouds, every star is falling.

All this happens.

She tries to see the boy in her mind. Tries to imagine his small body in Geoffrey's jacket. She wonders if her stockings are still in his pocket. She wonders where he is tonight and if she'll ever find him.

The rain has a voice. The rain answers. This rain says, *I have a body like yours and like your mother's. I have a body like your daughter's. I have a body. It's the boy's, and it's your sister's. They've stepped between the raindrops. They flow away. They're mostly water.*

N E C E S S A R Y

A N G E L S

⫻⫻⫻ DORA'S DISAPPEARED AGAIN. I see her lying in the field, in the abandoned refrigerator. She's not sleeping and she's not dead: she's between these places. And though I'm afraid for her even now, from this distance of years I can tell you Dora Stone is going to live.

The first time it happened, she was five years old, thirty-six pounds. While Mother dozed in the shade of her striped umbrella, Dora wandered up the beach, into the cool waves. She felt sand shifting under her feet, her small body sinking in the tug of an undertow. One man up the shore was close enough to save her. One fat white man burned red seemed to stare. But he didn't come. Was he blind behind his glasses, or was he curious, wanting to see what the child might do?

She wasn't that deep really. She wasn't going to drown. She was her own voice whispering in her own ear, *Just walk out.* Mother found her, safe and dry, so Lily's fury, stripped of fear, was pure, and the slaps were quick and hard, familiar — Dora knew how to let them fall: no crying, no ducking. The sting went away soon enough, and Mommy was sorry in the dark; Mommy came to Dora's room and lay down beside her in the blue bed. Mommy cried and held Dora, stroked her precious body, touched arm and neck and thigh as if to be sure the child was all there. She said, *What would Mommy do if she lost you?*

These are the bodies Lily's lost already: the husband with

another wife and two sons; the mother shrinking in the bed, wrinkling into the sheets till she was gone; the half-man down the hall, her father, lost; her own unknown self. She's not fat but blurred, lost in her body: drooping breasts and buttocks, spread white belly — lily-white Lily Stone, not a flower now though her skin is still petal soft and that pale, that easily bruised. Don't touch Mommy too hard, don't hug her too close, but she can touch you where and how she wants, can slap your head on the beach or swat your butt, can come to your room and lie beside you in your little bed, her breath wine sweet, her body a weight and heat that fills your room till you blur too, into her, *precious baby,* the place that is yourself and not yourself has disappeared, but you don't look at her here, and she's come to this room so many times you're not scared — why would you be scared of your own mother, who only wants to lie this close? Yes, it's hot, but you're used to that, so you let her sleep and do not tell her of waves or undertow, do not speak of sand, though you feel them in your body now, in your body that remembers everything, the pull and lick, the ground beneath you slipping. You do not speak of the burning man. He's yours. You keep these places to go alone: the water, the blind man's eyes, the stranger's hands.

The next time, Dora's six, tied in the closet, forgotten by twelve-year-old Max, her cousin and best friend, who has used his favorite knot, the Lazarus loop, so called because a person has roughly the same chance of escaping it as she has of rising from the dead.

It will happen again. Dora's bike is in the reeds by the canal. But eight-year-old Dora is gone. Or she's eleven, drunk on beer with Max, who is no longer allowed in their grandfather's house. They dance in the back of the truck, radio blaring, doors flung open, yellow light spilling into the swamp. The man in the song says he's a razor he's a rifle he's the water and Max says, *You're dangerous, girl.* Hours later, in the still dark, Dora wakes groggy and mystified on her own front lawn.

In the morning she'll learn of the stolen truck, Max's escape from the Alpena School for Boys, a string of gas stations robbed from Michigan to Florida and one attendant shot in the hand, *So if you know, little girl, you better tell us where.* Armed and dangerous, sweet tender Max, shaved almost bald — Max, whose dirty fingers snarled your long hair when he pulled you close. You should have known.

She's seven, she's twelve, she's fourteen, she's gone.

I see a dark-skinned boy on a bike riding toward the refrigerator in the field. He doesn't know what's in it, but he spots the silver bicycle sparkling in the grass. He can't believe what he finds. He's only a child, but he knows she's dangerous to him. He doesn't check for breath or pulse, doesn't lean close to see she's just a girl. He's smart enough not to touch. He flies across the field, pumping harder than he thought he could while the sun blazes and spits in the bleached white sky.

I'm Dora. I'm the girl in the refrigerator. I'm the girl in the closet. I'm the girl who's left her bike in the reeds by the canal. I can't be found.

I know you're afraid of where I'm going when I tell you this. I'm afraid. But I can't stop. Forgetting is the first lie, a little death. I won't abandon myself piece by piece. I know what happens to wicked runaway girls. You find us in rivers of grass, or floating in ponds. You find us under our own beds or stuffed in the hedges of our own yards. You find our shoes in trash heaps. When we surface at last, you give numbers to our bones. But this isn't one of those stories. See, these are my hands. This is my voice talking. As long as you hear me, I'm alive.

One night my father forgot to come home. Max forgot the boy with the bullet in his palm, forgot a woman pushed from her truck to the road. Max says, *I never did nothin' wrong.* My grandfather sits in the wheelchair upstairs, touching his right hand with his left, trying to remember when his body had two sides and the words that might explain. Mother says, *Just a bad dream, baby.*

They leave me to remember it all.

These are the rules:
  Don't sit in the sun.
  Don't ride your bike on the road.
  Don't walk by the canal.
Everything here is dangerous: heat, wind, days of rain — this water wants to rise, wants to take back this ground; waves want to splinter boats and wash dark bodies to the shore. Grass cuts your hand if you grab it; leaves tipped with poison pierce your clothes. The alligator in the sun looks harmless as rubber, a truck's blown tire, only the eyes moving, but one flick of the tail and you'll be in the water, your legs broken, your back numb.

But Dora always disobeyed; Dora always walked home along the canal. Even the ducks were fierce. She swatted at them with a stick. One bit her cheek — see, beneath the eye, this white scar.

Grandpa said, *Go get my gun.* He hated the ducks. Their noise. Their shit on his lawn. Dora promised to stay on the road, but he said, *Actions have consequences.* She knows she is the consequence of certain actions for which her mother is to blame. She knows she can't stop him now. This has nothing to do with her, the wound on the cheek, the eye that could have been lost. This is the voice of the gun, the stutter in the brain, the trembling hand, a hurt so old it's hard and small as the bullet in the heart of the gun.

She knows where it is, exactly, where it stands in the closet, propped against the wall — the clean, oiled, loaded rifle. She knows already how it feels in her small hands — exactly how long, how smooth. She knows its surprising weight.

Her grandfather once dreamed cities into being — the straight grids of streets, the safe repetition of houses — raised them out of wet ground. Now he speaks with a stutter; his walk is a stutter too. He's had one stroke already, will have six more before he dies, so Dora's mother says, *He couldn't have killed the ducks,* but Dora remembers the heavy bodies of birds falling from the sky.

And she remembers the girl. The moon was new, a carved blade slung low at twilight, reflected in water. She wanted to dive through it, into the rippling shadows of palms, wanted to swim away from her grandfather, whose hand was hot, whose whole body smelled of the swamp. But she was more afraid of the canal: reeds to wrap ankle and wrist, mud to suck you down.

This is why her grandfather dragged her here. This is what she saw. A pale girl in dark water. Floating. Face down.

Her grandfather squeezes her hand so tight her face goes numb.

This is her proof: her own feet cut by the shells embedded in the road. Fine scars now.

A dream, Mother says. *Yes, a girl did drown, but your grand-father was in a wheelchair by then, so how could he take you to the canal?*

Dora can't ask him. He doesn't know.

She's the only one who remembers how the water looked that night, smooth and slow, its surface tight as skin and just as fragile. How the girl's body seemed not to have fallen. She rose. She broke the skin. She was the white scar on the black surface of memory. Whether she existed or not, she was the place you entered if you wanted to remember it all.

This part Dora doesn't remember — she can't, she wasn't there. So she doesn't know how the boy who found her in the refrigerator told nobody all day, how he hid instead under his own porch, hoping that what he'd seen wasn't real, that he'd wake and forget. His mother stood at the door calling his name. The earth was dark, the sky still blue. The third time, her voice broke him, and the child crawled out.

He talks his way backward till he sees more at dusk than he saw in the scorched field. He knows now she's only a girl, very white but burned red, almost blistering, her eyelids — Did he come that close? Yes, now he remembers — and her thighs streaked with dirt — no, not dirt, something dry, rust-colored, flaking off her skin.

His mother is afraid for him in a new way, not afraid as she was when she stood alone and her son was only her voice, an image in her mind, the shape of her lips in the dark — now he's here, with her, in her arms, dirty, whole, but she's afraid because she wonders what they'll think when he tells them, *It's been hours.* She hears herself pleading, *He's only eight years old.* She wants to hide under the porch with him and wait till dawn — she's a mother, after all — but she sees the girl, those sore eyes. She believes in grace and knows this child, like hers, might be alive.

Dora doesn't remember how the boy led dogs and men back to the field in the now complete dark, doesn't remember how they questioned him, how they tried to make him conjure somebody else in that field, tried to make him believe that man's face was dark and familiar and this was the reason for his silence.

And she doesn't remember the hands under her, the hands on her chest pumping, the mouth on her mouth breathing, doesn't remember her body lifted to the stretcher, the white ambulance, the mask over nose and mouth, the needle jabbed in the vein and taped to the hand, doesn't remember the long white hall or the cool metal of the scissors cutting her out of her clothes, doesn't remember all the hands on her, where they touched and how.

Remembers only this: waking in the white room and her mother there asleep in the chair beside her, her mother opening her eyes at the same moment Dora opened hers, and in this way she thought her mother must know what had happened but won't say now or ever what it was, will only refer to it in the future as the time Dora rode her bike too long in the sun, the time Dora passed out and nearly died in the heat — and hadn't she been warned?

She doesn't feel anything inside. Feels only her burned skin. She would tell her mother something if she knew where to start.

Imagine this: another boy, not the one who will find her. None of that has happened yet. This one's no boy really and no stranger. *Lewis Freyer.* Like *prayer*, Dora thinks — when she remembers her hands on him it's that quiet.

Estrelle, who is his mother, used to come twice a week to clean the house, and Lewis came too sometimes until Estrelle caught them: filthy, together. Now she comes every day to take care of Dora's grandfather. She has a mother of her own at home, an old woman in a chair but not a wheelchair —

they don't have money for that — and anyway, Lewis is strong
enough to lift her anywhere she needs to go. She was six feet
tall, a prison guard, and now she's only four feet long, got one
wooden leg and one stump, and if there's any sense in that
Estrelle doesn't know. Dora's never seen her, has only heard
Estrelle talk. For years Estrelle has walked to and from this
house, across fields and roads, a mile and a half each way, but
Estrelle's not a young woman, you know, and lately her feet
have been bothering her, swollen and a bit numb, and this is
how her mother's troubles started, so now Lewis brings her in
the morning, returns for her in the afternoon.

He's sullen. No matter how hot it is, he stays in the gold
Impala. He won't come out for iced tea or lemonade, won't sit
in the shade, won't answer Dora when she says, *You're melting, Lewis.*

He sits like a deaf man, refuses to wipe his face though the
sweat trickles into ears and eyes, though the salt burns. Yes,
he's melting, but he can sit still as plaster and stare through
the skinny white girl.

Dora says, *You go too long without blinking, your eyes gonna
dry up and fall out of your skull.*

Still nothing — as if he's forgotten how they crawled
through culverts under roads, snagged their clothes on barbed
wire, fell down in the field alone.

He's a grown man, eighteen years old, so he can't remember
the weight of her small body on his, her dirty hand over his
mouth. Remembers only this: Estrelle in the yard, Estrelle
descending — *I'm gonna beat your black skin blue* — remembers that the seven-year-old girl who's now fourteen was the
reason for this and other shame.

Silent as he is, Dora persists. It's hot. She's bored. Nobody
but Estrelle has come to the house all summer. Nobody but

the skittish boy with festering skin who brings groceries and cases of wine to the back door. Nobody but the Haitian gardener with his whirring blades who carves the hedges, trims the lawn, every day. She could ride down the road, swim a hundred laps in a tiny pool while two other girls her age, her friends, lie greased and golden in the blistering sun. But she'd rather wait here, with him.

On the twelfth day, he speaks.

He says, "What the fuck do you want?"

After all her pestering, she doesn't know. "Nothing," she says, and for three days doesn't go near the car. Then he's the one to tempt her. She's on the porch, and he gets out of the Impala, so she sees him, really, for the first time — a man, thin but hard, all long muscle, dark in the bright sun.

This Lewis, who grins, who says, "I am thirsty," who takes the lemonade in his big hand and drinks it all in one pull, this Lewis who gives her the empty glass, leaves her mute. It's his hands that silence her, the way they flutter like wings opening so she sees the pale undersides marked with fine dark lines. This Lewis who squints, who almost scowls, makes her feel ashamed of her small body. She hears Lily say, *Don't talk to strangers. Don't stand in the sun.* She hears Grandpa: *Go get the gun.* The heavy-bodied birds drop from the sky, and Max whispers, *You're dangerous, girl.* It must be true, because even though she never said a word, Max, her sweetheart, her first love, was caught again.

Lewis says, "You meet me up the road I'll take you for a ride someday." She says she can't, and he laughs but it's mean. He says, "I thought you liked me."

She thinks of Max in jail, Max blaming her all these years, dangerous eleven-year-old Dora getting him drunk.

She says, "It's not what you think."

Lewis is sliding his long body into the gold Impala; he's closing the door slowly, a deliberate softness, he's whispering his words so she has to lean close; he's saying, *Tell me what I think.*

"Tomorrow," she says. And though she's afraid of what she'll do to him, she can't stop what they've begun.

They make love in her grandfather's car parked in the dark garage. They make love in the gold Impala at the end of a deserted road. They can't be seen together. They know this but never speak of it. They find a refrigerator in a field, a white box, a home, and they lie down but it's much too small. They remember childhood paths through woods and swamp, under barbed wire, over walls. Lewis knows how to come at night into the huge dark house, which door she's left unlocked; he knows how to be a shadow among shadows moving through the long halls, how to breathe as the house breathes, how to find Dora in the blue room in the soft bed, how to slip his hand over her mouth so she won't cry out, how to move like water through her and out of her, how to flow down the dark stairs into the dark yard before gathering himself into the hard shape of a man. *Go get the gun.* There's nobody here to say it now, nobody but the old man with half a face, the old man who can't get out of bed alone, who lies like a bug on his back till morning when Estrelle comes. There's nobody here but the mother fallen across the couch, snoring in wine-thick sleep. Nobody here but little Dora in the damp bed.

Tonight he lifted his grandmother, carried her from the chair where she sits all day to the couch where she sleeps. Even without her legs she's a big woman, heavy. She never leaves this house, but she sees far beyond these walls. She feels the heat of the boy's skin where he touches. She knows. She says, *You watch yourself, Lewis.* She says, *Your mama's had all the sorrow she can bear.*

He would never tell Dora, would never name his mother's grief, would never describe the three rooms where he lives with her and her mother and two sisters, the kitchen table where he and his sisters and brother were born, would never try to explain what it means to be the youngest child of seven and the only man in the house.

But somehow she knows. She imagines the old woman in his arms, knows that despite her losses she weighs more than Dora ever will, that this weight is a thing he carries every time he climbs the stairs of her house.

He does not find her pretty in any way. She has a flat butt, barely swollen breasts. The thick blue veins roping her thin arms seem unnatural on a girl so small. Her blond hair is clipped short, dyed black, but comes in yellow at the roots. In any light she looks too naked, not just stripped but skinned.

He's had girls before. Women, he calls them. They knew what to do. They had red mouths, quick hands. They were never this naked. They were wet and open, their bodies full and safe and soft. They had rubbers in their purses. He could meet them anywhere, anytime. No one had to lie.

He and Dora never talk. They know everything and nothing; they're bound: his mother combs her grandfather's hair, clips his nails, wipes his bum. She's more than wife or daughter ever was. What the old man feels for Estrelle is his secret but will never be as fragile or forgettable as love.

The blue car.

The stifling heat of the garage.

He says, "Does it scare you?"

She knows he means his body, how long it is, how dark, and she thinks of her mother climbing out of the tub, all that flesh rushing toward her, loose breasts flapping, dimpled thighs whispering where they rub — she thinks of her grandfather grabbing with his one good hand, the thumbprint of bruise he leaves — she thinks of the cheek she's supposed to kiss, the rough white-whiskered skin — she imagines these familiar bodies, how they make her forget what's her and not her, how she's terrified of the place they blur.

Where Lewis touches, he defines — dark hand on white rib. So she's not afraid. But he is — afraid of these frail ribs. He can rest his long fingers in the spaces between them — she's that thin, and her skin too, so fine he feels he might put his hand through her. He would not say he loves her or even likes her. If he could explain it at all, he might say it is this fear that makes him tender, this fear that brings him to the house again and again — he sees her brittle ribs as the rigging of a tiny boat rocking on black water; it is this sound, waves lapping wood, that calls him. Small and breakable as the girl is, the body he enters is a way out.

Tonight Dora's grandfather could not be comforted. He rolled around and around the room, using his cane to move the chair with his strong left hand. He dumped the drawers, looking for something that can't be found. He refused to understand who Lily was, and finally she left him, locked him in the room so he wouldn't propel himself down the hall, so he wouldn't fly down the stairs. He banged the wheels of his chair against the door. He rattled the knob. When his yell broke to a whimper, it was Estrelle's name he called.

Dora tells Lewis none of this. She wants to be her body only, her body in the car, in the rain, out here on the black road. But her body is a map. Her body is a history. His fingers find every scar and bruise. *What happened here, and here?* He doesn't ask, but where he touches she remembers. She cries, and he holds her. He expects no explanation. He isn't scared of sorrow. It doesn't surprise him. When he's calmed her, he touches her again.

She imagines her grandfather upstairs in the house far from this road. He's rolled his chair close to the window. He's trying to see through the rain, trying to remember his right shoulder, how the raised rifle kicked as he fired. He's trying to count the ducks falling from the sky, but there are too many, they always come too fast, and then he sees, he understands this one thing: it's only the rain.

She imagines Lewis's grandmother — one stump, one wooden leg; Lewis is touching her legs — and she sees her own future, her body coming apart, how she'll lose it piece by piece. She doesn't know how he does this to her, why he won't stop. They make love so many times, so long, her fingers and feet and lips go numb.

They will be caught. It's necessary. They know this as they know each other: without words. They are waiting in their silence to see how it will happen.

The gold Impala, empty.
   A dirt road.
   Tonight they saw the pretty little horses, the setting sun.
   Four ponies, lean and glowing in the gold light. One deep ginger with hair like velvet. One the bleached white of bone.

Two bays nuzzling. They heard the hum of insect wings, saw the ginger pony brace his legs to piss hard.

Later they stood on a bridge, watching gulls swoop high, then dive toward water, saw them vanish at the surface as if a blue hole opened between air and river.

Tonight when they lay down in the woods where palm and pine grow together, they touched each other's bones: hips, cheeks, spine. Tonight, for the first time, they closed their eyes and almost slept, the man enfolding the child, one bird fallen — her body the white belly, his the dark wings — and it is in this way they wake to the sound of glass shattering on the road.

It's only boys, three of them, nine or ten years old.

They beat the car with sticks and rocks. Lewis knows that if he closes his eyes the bare-chested boys with sticks will become men with guns. He lies naked, watching children destroy the car. His hand clamps Dora's mouth, and she wonders, Does he think I'm fool enough to yell? It's not that simple, his fear. What he wants is for the body beneath his body to be gone. But her body insists. Still as it is, it is too many sharp bones. It will not soften, will not be hidden, will not sink into this ground. The boys jab their little knives into tires; the air escaping hisses off the road. His body hot on top of hers has a smell of something smoldering, about to burn, and then the match is struck, the first one, and the vinyl seats are split open with the sharp knives and the stuffing spills out — the first match is thrown and the second match is struck and the smell in the night is melting plastic. Together, two boys stand on the hood to drop a rock onto the windshield, and the glass is a shattered web caved in that does not break apart. Black smoke billows from open doors. The man in the woods has pressed the air from the girl's lungs, and the

boys, who are thrilled with their miraculous destruction, are
mounting their bikes and peddling home.

He is off her and she gulps air. He hates the boys, their bare
white skin, their whoops and their strange silence in the end,
but they're gone, so it's only the girl beside him now, silent but
for her gasping, and he hates that sound, and he hates her
bright reflecting skin — he can't see his own hand at the end
of his own arm.

He wants her dressed, and she knows; she's quick. He
wants to leave her or be able to love her despite everything.
But he can't escape the smell of fear, strong as piss, rising
from his skin. He can't escape the rage, a shaking too deep to
stop, blood quivering in the veins. He wants to weep, thinking
of his mother in the morning, walking to this girl's house.

There's nothing to do but let the car burn. The sky's gone
green with clouds. If the storm comes soon enough, if the
rain's hard, these flames might flicker out.

They walk together partway and then alone. They do not
touch or speak. They do not look over their shoulders. They do
not look up and hope.

When he disappears, he disappears completely, moving
across the field, silent and invisible as the black canal. She
thinks he is gone forever. She leaves no door unlocked. But
that night he comes again.

He's green sky and wind. He swirls up from the south.

He's the wind uprooting palms, pavement that seems to
melt and flow, the drone of pumps. He's three stones hitting
the glass of her window, sharper than rain. He's all sound.

She's afraid of him but more afraid for him, his new reck-
lessness and what would happen if her mother woke and made

one call? What would anyone see here but a dark-skinned man at a white girl's door? So she's opening the window, letting the rain pour in — she's speaking his name into the wind and he hears her — she's moving down the stairs to open the door so carefully locked.

He's inside, he's there, filling the doorway, dripping, dark, his clothes drenched, his skin wet, his hair full of rain. Water flows from him, puddles on the floor; muddy rivulets stream across the tile, and Dora thinks of Estrelle on her hands and knees tomorrow, Estrelle not asking, not her business what the white people do in their own house, just her business to make it right when they stop.

She's wearing a long T-shirt, her underpants. Nothing else. She's cold. But it's not cold. Her shaking is a spasm now, in her chest and knees. She leans against the door so she won't fall. She says, *Why are you here?* He moves close and she smells his breath and body, the burn of adrenaline, the acid rising in his throat. He grabs her wrist, pulls up his wet shirt to press her palm to his stomach. *Can you feel it?* he says. He means the quivering, the blood jumping under the skin — he believes she'll know. But she doesn't know.

He says, *I have to lie down.*

She thinks he wants to hurt her still. His body's hard against her — belly, hip, hand — hard. His fingers twist her hair and pull. She remembers the weight of him in the woods. He squeezes her bare arm, says again, *I have to lie down.* He says, *I want this to stop.*

He's following her up the stairs. He's leaving his muddy tracks through her house but he doesn't care — it's the last time, he's not coming back. So what if the doors are chained and bolted after this, what if there are big-headed dogs in the yard after this, what if the girl is slapped and questioned till she spits out a lie or the ridiculous, unbelievable truth, what does he care?

In the blue room, on the blue bed, he strokes her body through the shirt; he strokes her bare thighs. She wants him to hate her. She wants him to do this and be gone — she wants to lie on the bed alone while the wind tears the palms out of the ground, while the rain blown sideways batters the house — she wants nothing left of him but the damp place where he lay in his wet clothes. She wants him not to kiss, not to touch her face, not to put his fingers in her mouth; she wants him not naked, only unzipped — quick, hard — she wants to hate him and be hurt and be done. She wants him not to speak ever again. She wants not to feel the short blades, not to hear the hiss of air, not to smell the vinyl melting on his skin.

But he is naked. He's pulled the T-shirt over her head. He's pulled the panties down to her ankles. She's small in this room, in this bed, a child in this house, herself and not herself — she's letting him touch her, everywhere — he's inside her, everywhere, and it's wrong, she knows, to want him and be this scared. She thinks of the grandfather down the hall, wide-eyed and helpless in his bed. She imagines he knows everything and wants to come but can't come. She imagines him weeping, longing to put his big hands on the smooth gun. And the man in this bed is kissing her eyelids. His long fingers are in her mouth. She's terrified, and he knows and he holds her head in both hands and he moves so slowly, and his lips are almost touching hers when he whispers, *Baby, no,* and she sees she's herself again, not blurred with the boys on the road; she's his lover, and that's what breaks her and breaks him, because they see the muddy tracks through this house, because they can follow those footsteps back along a muddy road to a place where a gold car exploded hours ago and is burning still — it's a fire the rain can't put out.

He wants to go. He's pulling on his wet clothes. She knows how it ends here. He won't risk this again, for her. The boys in their bright skin will dance around this bed forever. The gold flames will rise forever from the road.

He's his own footprints wiped from the stairs. He's the rose-splattered bedspread washed and dried. He's the faint outline only she can find.

But it's not over.

It's just begun.

Hard as he tries to go, there's no way out of her. Not long now till she'll know. First the swelling. Then the sickness and no blood. *Actions have consequences.* Your grandfather can't say it now, but it doesn't matter: you know who can't help you, who can't be called. And the consequence of no action is to understand what you'll do alone.

It's easy to steal what you need. You don't ask yourself what's right. You think of boys with sticks and Max in jail, how dangerous you are, rocks thrown at your window, a wet man who flows through you: first rain, then fire. You imagine your life forever in this house.

There's cash in Lily's purse, wads of it, uncounted — for Estrelle and the gardener, for any shy boy who might bring wine to the back door. You know how much to take each week for four weeks. You know how soon and where to go. Seven miles. It's not that far. You ride your bike. You don't think what you'll do after. *After* is another country, a place you can't know.

The woman at the desk counts your money, says, *Age?*,

squints when you say *Eighteen* but writes it down. She says, *How will you get home?* And Dora says her boyfriend will come; he's got a car and all she has to do is call, and the woman Dora won't remember says, *That's fine, but we can't let you go till somebody comes,* and Dora nods, of course, somebody will come.

There's the finger to be pricked and one drop of blood. There's a movie and a clever girl who shows you the pink model of your uterus, who explains what she calls *the procedure.* There's the yellow pill to calm you and seven colored birds hanging from the ceiling, twisting on their strings over the table. There's the clever girl in green scrubs now, offering two fingers for you to grip. She says, *You can't hurt me.* And the doctor comes in his white mask. He's a face you won't know and don't want to know, and he says, *You're a little one;* he's already between your legs, so you're not sure what he means, but you can squeeze too hard, and the girl says, *Let go.* The sound is water in a vacuum. The paper birds spin. The curved blade is quick, and the doctor says, *That's all.*

In a room with tiny windows too high there are eleven beds; you are number eight. You eat cookies, drink juice — obedient Dora, you hold out your arm, let one more woman in green take the pressure of your blood, ninety over sixty, a lie, what could they know about your blood? A third woman tells you to rest now, just for an hour, don't move — here's a pad, your underwear, call me if there's too much blood.

How much is too much?

How many times do the little boys jab their knives into soft tires?

How many matches make a car explode?

She's too weak to do what she needs to do. She drifts and wakes. A woman's whispering, *We've got a bleeder.* Dora hopes it's not her. She feels the stabbing from inside, the doctor again, the bright boys. It could be her. She checks her underwear, sees the black clots, the thin red streaks — not too much — there's so much more blood in a body than this — and the woman who is the bleeder is screaming now, feeling the blood beneath her, slippery, the blood, and the three women in green hold her down.

Dora sees and takes her one chance, gathers her clothes in a ball, slips from the bed and out the door.

In the bathroom she wads the paper gown in the trash with the soaked pad. She stuffs paper towels in her underpants. She doesn't look. What good would it do to know? Her shoes are in the other room where the woman has stopped wailing.

The window here is wide enough, and Dora Stone is gone.

I see her on the road, riding. I know it's true but still don't quite believe she's doing this. She's dizzy. She can't sit down. The air rises in waves off the pavement. It's not the heat but the light she can't bear. She weaves and cars honk, but nobody stops and the sound of horns is a distant sound to her, a sound from her life, before. She can't see anything except her own hands on the bike, gleaming metal, and the road moving under her. She means to go home, but it's too far, and she goes to the field instead, lies in the refrigerator instead, and this is where the things she can't remember begin:

the boy on the bike
the mother on the porch
the dogs in the dark
their smell, her smell
and then the men
the needle, the mask, the scissors gliding along her skin.
This is where you wake in a white room. This is where the

mother, your mother, opens her eyes at exactly the same moment you open yours.

You do not think of God or mercy. You think of water, cows and trailers swirling across flooded lawns; you think of wind, the furious swaying heads of palms in the moments before they fall; you think of your grandfather's cities, the ones he built and can't remember now, the cities where streets flow with mud and hail, rivers of forgetfulness, and the roofless identical houses split open, walls and rafters splinter on the ground; you think of boats, their crammed cargo, arms and legs dangling over rails, torsos twisting, all those dark bodies straining toward this shore.

Now it's the blue room at night, and Estrelle stands in the corner, and Dora thinks she should have gone home hours ago, and why does she stand there, and Estrelle says, *Don't you ever tell.*

She thinks he comes again. She thinks he's a scatter of stones, but it's only rain. She thinks he must know what's happened to her body, how she's forever changed. But only Estrelle comes, only Estrelle speaks. *Boys like mine still rising out of the swamps because of ignorant girls like you.*

He who's touched her everywhere, who touches her now, who's asked with his silent hands what happened here and here — green bruise, white scar — he who's seen her body in every light, touched her body in every dark place, whose fingers brush her lips like moth wings, he never comes.

He's lying in his bed and she can't believe he doesn't feel the hard table beneath them, doesn't see the paper birds, doesn't ride and ride and then lie down forever in the white box, doesn't lie down to burn in the field with her.

It's September. Dora Stone is still fourteen, starting ninth grade. She trims the dark ends of her hair, lets it grow back blond. She visits friends. She swims in tiny turquoise pools. She drinks rum and orange juice like the other girls. A glass shatters on concrete. She laughs at her own stupid hands, her own foot bleeding.

Dora's sixteen, and Estrelle's in the kitchen crying, saying her poor mama's dead at last and Lewis going to be married next week, moving north with his pretty wife, baby coming a little bit soon but not too soon, and Lewis gonna get that training, be an EMT like he always wanted. *Did he?* Dora doesn't know. Think of it, her boy, saving lives every night, and yes she's worried and yes she'll miss him but mostly she's proud. Estrelle's in the blue room in the middle of the night. She's got her hand over Dora's mouth. Grandfather's had the seventh stroke. The wind blows the curtains over the bed; the woman's gone.

There's a man on the television. Mugged having a heart attack. Detroit. *Lewis, is this where you are?* Revived by an off-duty EMT. *Did you save him? Did you rip his shirt, put your hands on his chest, your mouth on his mouth?*

Dora's twenty. She lives alone, has left her mother forty miles north in the big house, alone. She has a job.

Collecting urine.

Taking blood.

Everybody in this city is terrified: the men with big veins, the women with no hair, the little girls pissing in jars. Nobody wants to find out. She knows what to do. She knows how scared they are, that later, when they know for sure, they'll be hurt all the time. So she's careful with the needle and the rubber hose. She doesn't want to hurt them now.

She's had lovers, a string of them, a parade — the serial lovers, she calls them, one after another. She's dangerous still — this body, this skin, this blood — *don't touch me if you don't want to know.* But they do touch. They come and go. They pass through her and under her. They pin her down.

Sometimes she thinks he'll come the way the others come. They're muddied reflections in black water — they're imprints in white sand — they're mouths opening in the rain — her lovers — they're a line of men in white masks and white gowns — they're the wrinkled sheets — they're naked boys. They want her to lie down.

He thinks he was the one in danger. You could argue with him now. You could show him your rubber gloves, the vials of blood, the spit in the sink, the warm yellow fluid trembling in the glistening jars. You could tell him how careful you are at work, how careless at home. You could tell him how it felt on the hard table, on the long ride, in the refrigerator, in the dark room, how it was through the days of silence that followed and now through the years of fear when you think this will happen again and again — to your body alone — this will keep happening until one day, one day you really will be gone. You could tell him how terrifying it is to live in your bright skin. You could make him touch the place it still burns. You could touch him. You could open his veins. You could drink his blood. You could tell him the one thing that matters now: *Listen, it won't be that long — unknown and unforgiven as I am, I want to live in my body somehow.* You could ask him who he saved tonight. You could make him tell you what he sees when he closes his eyes and the heart beneath his hands starts to beat again.